A Good Man Is
Hard to Find

A GOOD MAN IS HARD TO FIND

ReShonda Tate Billingsley

THORNDIKE PRESS

A part of Gale, Cengage Learning

GALE
CENGAGE Learning·

Detroit • New York • San Francisco • New Haven, Conn • Waterville, Maine • London

GALE
CENGAGE Learning

LIBRARY OF CONGRESS CATALOGING-IN-PUBLICATION DATA

Billingsley, ReShonda Tate.
    A good man is hard to find / by ReShonda Tate Billingsley.
      p. cm.
    ISBN-13: 978-1-4104-4014-3 (hardcover)
    ISBN-10: 1-4104-4014-1 (hardcover)
    1. Women journalists—Fiction. 2. Women singers—Fiction. 3. Aruba—Fiction. 4. Swindlers and swindling—Fiction. 5. Large type books. I. Title.
    PS3602.I445G66 2011
    813'.6—dc22   2011018950

Published in 2011 by arrangement with Gallery Books, a division of Simon & Schuster, Inc.

Printed in Mexico
1 2 3 4 5 6 7 15 14 13 12 11

To the good men of the world . . .
You know who you are . . .

A NOTE FROM THE AUTHOR

I am so blessed to have enjoyed a wonderful career writing faith-based fiction. But as a writer who is always trying to further develop her craft, I wanted to spread my wings. I wanted to try something I'd never done before, and since I love suspense with a dash of romance, I decided that was where my wings should take me next. And since I love to travel (but seldom get to do so), I also thought: What better way to combine all the things I love than to write the book you now have in your hands.

When I began to explore what topic I would focus on, I immediately thought of the adage "write what you know." I happen to know what being a tabloid reporter is like. Yes, I was one. I was the paparazzi (shhh, don't tell anyone). I won't say which tabloid I worked for, but let's just say it was an eye-opening experience. The job was challenging, sometimes fun, but at the end of the day, it was not for me (not to mention the fact that my mom was so embarrassed by where I worked that she told people I worked for a top-secret government agency). So, I moved on, back to mainstream journalism. But I'm happy to revisit that tabloid world with the characters in this book.

If you're one of my regular readers, I hope you'll give this book a chance. If you're a new reader, welcome to my world. I hope you enjoy the ride.

Of course, before I go, I have to take a moment to say thank you to those who helped make this book happen.

As usual, my first ounce of gratitude is for God, who gave me the talent to tell tales. To my wonderful, patient, understanding family, I can't thank you enough for bearing with me as I ventured into new territory.

To my sister-friends, whether I talk to you every day or once every other month, I take comfort in knowing you are there for me.

Of course, many, many thanks to the people who make up my literary life — my agent, Sara Camilli; my assistant, Tasha Martin; my editor, Brigitte Smith; my other editor, John Paine; my publicist, Melissa Gramstad; my publisher, Louise Burke; and everyone else at Simon & Schuster/Gallery

Books, thank you for everything!

To my writer friends . . . those hanging on and those struggling to survive . . . keep writing! No matter how many iPads, iPhones, BlackBerrys, Kindles, e-readers, et cetera, dominate our lives, the world will always be in need of a good book.

To all the bookstores, book clubs, libraries, and online communities that have supported my work, I hope you'll do the same with this book.

Until the next book. . . . Enjoy!

Much love,
ReShonda

1

Your days are numbered . . .

The slightly wrinkled paper trembled in her hand. The words were written in big, bold stencil letters. Normally, Ava Cole blew off such threats. After all, as an investigative reporter who had built a solid reputation for bringing down corrupt politicians and businessmen, she had no shortage of people who would like to see her head on a platter. Usually, though, they were just harmless disgruntled people who understood that at the end of the day, she was simply doing her job. But this was the fourth message she'd received in the past two weeks.

Your days are numbered . . .

"Excuse me, are you all right?"

Ava jumped when she felt a hand on her shoulder. She spun around to see a tall, muscular man standing over her. He had light brown eyes and wore his dark hair cut low and neatly trimmed. He looked ruggedly handsome in a pair of jeans and a New York Knicks jersey.

"What did you say?" Ava said.

"I said, are you all right?" he repeated with a look of genuine concern.

Ava shook herself out of her daze. She recognized the man from somewhere, but she couldn't remember where. Was he the letter-writing type?

"Yeah, I'm . . . I'm fine," she stammered, instinctively pulling the paper close to her. A homeless man had walked up to her as she returned from her lunch break, thrust the letter in her hand, then darted off.

"You don't look fine," he replied.

"Well, I am," she snapped as she quickly stuffed the note down into her purse, out of sight.

The man took a step back, raising his hands in innocence. "Whoa, I didn't mean to get you upset. It's just that you look like you've seen a ghost."

"No, I'm fine," Ava said. In fact, she was quite rattled, but she didn't need to share her fears with someone she didn't know.

"Well, I didn't mean to pry into your affairs. I was just walking by and noticed the distressed look on your face."

Ava hadn't even realized she was standing

on the sidewalk in front of her office building, looking petrified. "Well, I'm fine, okay?" She didn't bother hiding her aggravation.

He was looking at her like she had escaped from a mental hospital. "Okay, you're fine." He sighed. "Maybe I should start over. I'm Clifton Edwards, but my friends call me Cliff." He extended his hand.

Ava didn't bother taking it. "Thank you for your concern, *Clifton.*" She shifted her purse to her other shoulder. "But you can go spy on someone else."

Ava wasn't normally a rude person, but this letter had her nerves on edge. Each one she'd received talked about her dying. In the past she'd gotten letters telling her to go to hell, or calling her every name under the sun. She'd even had a couple wishing her ill will, but nothing ever like this.

"Ava, isn't it?" he said as she brushed past him.

She sighed, wishing he would just go away. "Yes, it's Ava." She turned back to face him. He seemed perfectly nice. There really was no need to be nasty to him. "Ava Cole," she said, smiling.

"I work there," he said, pointing to the tall glass edifice next to her office building. They were connected by a glass skyway, but she seldom ventured over to that side. "At

13

the *National Star,*" he continued.

Ava couldn't stop a disgusted look from crossing her face.

He smiled like he was used to that reaction. "Well, it's obvious you're fine. I just wanted to make sure." He backed away. "You have a good day," he added as he walked off.

Ava debated stopping him just to apologize for her behavior, but she needed to get going. She was late for a very important meeting with her boss. *I'll apologize to him some other time,* she thought as she hurried inside the building. Her boss had sent her a text saying she needed to come see him as soon as she got back from her lunch break. She'd run over to a shoe sale at Saks with her girlfriend, and even though she hadn't bought anything, it had taken a lot longer than she'd expected.

Ava made up her mind that she would turn this letter over to the police. She hadn't reported the others, but her gut was telling her it was time. Four was getting to be excessive.

Ava dropped her purse off at her desk, grabbed a cup of coffee, and headed to her boss's office. She took a seat in front of Sebastian Mourning's desk. "So, what's so urgent?"

Two minutes later, her mouth was hanging wide open.

"Tell me that this is some cruel, cruel joke," she muttered as she tried to process what Sebastian had just said.

He didn't crack a smile.

"Sorry, Ava, you know I like you. You're a damn good journalist, but it's either this or move you to doing the obituaries for the *New York News*," he said.

Ava stared at him in disbelief. "You want me to go work for a tabloid magazine? You want me to join the paparazzi?" She'd worked at the esteemed *Newswire* magazine for five years, and Sebastian actually expected her to go work for their sister publication, the tabloid magazine the *National Star*? Her thoughts flashed to Clifton — Cliff, she reminded herself.

"Don't say it like that," Sebastian quipped. "You're still a reporter."

"You can try to sugarcoat it all you want, but I'd be a tabloid reporter! I graduated from the Columbia School of Journalism and you want me to chase after celebrities?" she asked incredulously.

"I'm well aware of your credentials, Ava," Sebastian said, rubbing his temples. "But I'm not left with much choice. They're shutting down the investigative division here, so that means we are all being forced out. All of the media outlets are cutting out their investigative divisions, so the chances of you finding something else is slim to none." He sighed heavily. "Now, I'm taking the retirement package. It's time for me to get out of the game. No one cares about serious journalism anymore." He held up a folder. "These are all the folks that I have to let go altogether. At least we were able to find a spot to move you to." He dropped the folder onto his cluttered desk. "You can take the contract home and review it," he said, sliding a legal-size piece of paper toward her. "Take it or leave it."

Ava no doubt wanted to leave it. But then she thought about the seven-hundred-dollar-a-month note on her Lexus (even though she seldom drove it, she loved having her own car), the twenty-nine-hundred-dollar-a-month mortgage payment on her brownstone, and the countless other bills she'd stacked up since moving to New York five years ago. She knew she didn't have a choice — she had to take it.

"Don't look like that," Sebastian said, trying to sound comforting, although he wasn't succeeding. He released a sigh and slid another folder her way. "Your first gig is a doozy."

Ava groaned as she accepted the folder. "What, Elvis returned from the dead and got Michelle Obama pregnant? Oh wait, Martians have invaded the White House?"

"Joke all you want, this is your career now," he said matter-of-factly.

Ava rolled her eyes as she flipped the folder open. "India Wright?" She frowned as she stared at the eight-by-ten glossy of the country's hottest pop star. She was bigger than Beyoncé, had sold more records than Celine Dion, and was now blowing up the big screen as well as the charts. "Who is this?" Ava held up a picture of a model-handsome man that had been nestled behind India's picture. He gave new meaning to the term "tall, dark, and gorgeous."

Sebastian stood and started gathering things off his desk. "That's Fredericko de la Cruz, India's soon-to-be husband. Look, I'm cleaning out my office, then I'm going to get drunk with some old colleagues so we can remember the way things used to be back when we still pounded out the news on typewriters. Your new editor, Eli Lacy, will fill you in on all the details tomorrow. They just wanted me to get you started."

"Started on what?"

"Your assignment. India is getting married next week and you're all over it."

She jumped from her seat. "*A wedding? You want me to cover a wedding?*" He had to be kidding her. She'd won an Emmy for her exposé on a toxic waste plant. She'd been interviewed on CNN, MSNBC, and Fox for her coverage of the 2008 presidential election, and these people expected her to cover a *wedding?*

"I don't want you to do anything. Your new bosses do. And judging by the garbage" — he stopped himself — "umm, I mean, the stuff they put in that magazine, they want much more than a simple 'here comes the bride' story. They want some dirt. Something that will have the magazine flying off the shelves."

"And why do they think I'm the person to do it?"

He smiled for the first time since she'd stepped into his office. "You didn't win those Emmys for investigative journalism for nothing."

"What about my assignment today? I'm about to blow the whistle on that corrupt New Jersey banker. I meet with my contact over there this evening."

Sebastian shook his head. "Unless that contact can give you some insight into India's wedding, cancel it. As of today, there's no more investigate unit at *Newswire* magazine."

"But, Sebastian —"

He held up his hand to cut her off. "I feel your pain. I really do. But it's not my problem anymore." He looked at his watch. "As of four minutes and thirty-nine seconds ago, I am no longer employed by Rhodes News Corporation." He tossed a picture frame into a box. "Oh, screw it. I'll come back tomorrow and finish this. I need a drink." He looked at her sympathetically. "I'm sorry, Ava, but the ride is over." He paused, and a hint of his usual newsman's curiosity showed in his expression. "I will tell you this. India is hot, but she's hiding something. And they want you to find out what that is."

"But —"

"But, I suggest you do it. If anyone can dig it up, you can. You'll do it if you want to keep your job — your six-figure job — and I don't need to remind you that six-figure jobs are very hard to come by these days."

With that, Sebastian Mourning slung his coat over his shoulder and walked out of the office.

2

This had been the day from hell. After everything at work, as soon as she stepped off the subway, it started pouring, messing up her two-hundred-and-forty-dollar hairstyle. Ava was so disgusted that all she wanted to do was get home, collapse on the sofa, and have her fiancé, Phillip, massage her feet.

Ava unlocked her front door, then stood in the doorway of their small Harlem brownstone, watching Phillip. She wondered how long it would take before he even noticed her. What she wouldn't give to just fall into his arms and have him tell her everything was going to be all right. Yet they were long past that stage. After Ava had told Phillip about her first two threatening letters, he'd replied by telling her, "You shouldn't go around pissing people off." So much for comfort.

At one time, Phillip had been the love of

Ava's life. They'd met at a coffee shop three weeks after she'd moved to New York City and had immediately hit it off. That was five years ago. Now Ava's relationship with Phillip was contemptuous at best. All they did lately was fight. Probably because she was tired of being his fiancée. Ava wanted to be his wife.

That was a fight she was tired of having as well. She shouldn't have to beg any man to marry her, and that's the point they had reached, which was ironic because he was the one who'd proposed two and a half years ago. Ava would've never said yes if she had known her engagement would be indefinite. Every time she tried to get him to pin down a date, though, he gave her some lame excuse about the timing not being right. They'd had so many arguments about it that she didn't even bring it up anymore.

Phillip finally sensed her presence because he looked up from his seat on the sofa — a seat that Ava thought he had to be glued to since he never moved from it. His job had gone to a virtual office and cut back his hours. So when he did work, as a systems engineer, he occupied that very spot on the sofa. And when he wasn't working, he was watching TV.

"Why are you standing there in the door

like that?" he asked, annoyed.

Ava shut the door and walked in. "Well, hello to you, too," she snapped as she dropped her purse and briefcase on the end table.

"What has your panties in a bunch?" Ava couldn't help but note that he picked up the remote and paused the DVR. She shook her head. Heaven forbid he should miss one second of *CSI*.

"I've just had a really bad and really long day." She released a heavy sigh as she plopped down on the sofa next to him. He instinctively moved his laptop out of the way as his eyes remained glued to the TV like he really wanted to get back to his show.

"Ummm, well, why don't you go take a long, relaxing bath, then come tell me all about it?" he said.

Ava stared at him in disbelief. She had no doubt that he was dead serious. He was always pushing her away, and she knew how this would play out. When she did come back, he'd act like he was asleep or would be totally engrossed in something else and would blow her off. "You know, just once I'd like to be a priority in your life," she said.

Phillip rolled his eyes. "Oh, here we go with this again." He unpaused the TV.

"Since I know how this argument is going to turn out, why don't we skip it altogether? You go relax and take your bath. I'll order some Chinese food, then we can sit and talk."

Like that's going to happen, she thought. Ava couldn't remember the last time they'd just sat and talked. He'd moved in with her a year ago, right after they'd downsized his company. Their relationship had been going downhill ever since. But he had to get over his lackadaisical attitude just this once. She needed him to be there for her as she tried to figure out what to do next.

"Look," Ava began, "have you heard anything from your company about when or if they're going to bring you back full-time?"

He didn't bother looking her way. "No. Why?"

His lack of attention was driving her crazy. "Because my company shut down my division today!"

That caught his attention. He turned and stared at her. "What?"

"They closed down the investigative unit of the magazine." Ava was about to tell him the "but" part — that they were moving her to another magazine — but the expression on his face stopped her in her tracks. It wasn't one of concern over her well-being. He looked worried that he would have to go back to work full-time.

"What are you going to do?" he asked.

"Well, I was hoping that *we* could figure something out. Maybe you could support us for a change, while I try to find another job." She hadn't meant for that to come out like an accusation, but she was too tired to be polite.

"What is that supposed to mean?" he asked, offended, standing up.

Since she'd opened the door, she might as well walk through it. "It means it's been a year since you've been downsized and you've made no effort to find another job," she said, standing up to face him. "In the beginning, you used to help me with the bills. You don't even try anymore."

"So, you're saying I'm trifling?"

She folded her arms defiantly. "You said it. I didn't."

His eyes blazed with anger as they faced off. After a few moments he said, "I'm out of here. I don't have to take this."

She didn't try to stop him as he stormed out of the apartment. She wasn't too worried. He'd be back. He didn't have anyplace else to go.

As Ava made her way upstairs, she re-

24

flected on her relationship with Phillip. They hadn't always been so . . . she couldn't find the right words to describe what their relationship had morphed into. To be honest, it reminded her of her grandparents'. They'd been married forty years, and while she knew they loved each other, they merely coexisted. They watched separate TV shows, ate dinner separately, and literally came together only on Sunday mornings for church. That was definitely not a life she wanted for herself.

In her bedroom, Ava began removing her work clothes. She changed into a comfortable pair of lounging pants and a tank top, pulled her wet hair back into a ponytail, then stretched out across her bed. She pulled the legal-size piece of paper out of her leather briefcase and stared at it. It seemed to be taunting her, saying: "Either sign me or return back to your funky old hometown."

No, going back to Dermott, Arkansas, isn't an option. She had another year left on her student loans. She had almost paid off those credit cards that had had a choke hold on her since her junior year of college. Not to mention the money she sent home every month to her grandparents and the fact that she was all but supporting her younger sister, Mia, who had just graduated college and was living in Los Angeles, trying to break into the entertainment business as a personal assistant, a pursuit that made no sense to Ava. Who went to college to become a personal assistant?

Ava shook away those thoughts. She couldn't get sidetracked thinking about her flighty sister. The bottom line remained: Ava couldn't walk away from the money the scandal rag was offering. She had three writer friends who'd been looking for work for the last nine months. The recession had taken its toll on journalists and freelance writers, not to mention that print magazines were doing a swan dive in general. Ava didn't want to join their ranks. And she didn't have to. All she had to do was sign on the dotted line.

Her cell phone rang before she could pick up the pen. Ava sighed when she saw her sister's number. She pressed the Talk button. "Hello, Mia."

"Sissy!" Mia said in her perpetually bubbly voice. Ava could envision her sister heading down Rodeo Drive, wearing oversize sunglasses, a high-dollar outfit, and to-die-for shoes, her fabulous hair blowing in the wind. All an act, carefully crafted, Mia said, to show some star that she looked important enough to bring on her team.

"What's going on?" Ava asked.

"Jimmy," Mia sang.

"Jimmy? What does that mean?"

"Jimmy Choos are going on sale tomorrow morning at nine A.M., and I have to have these cute little gold pumps I've been eyeing. So I was hoping my big sissy could help me out."

Ava closed her eyes and sighed. "Mia, I am not sending you money for Jimmy Choos. I don't even own a pair of Jimmy Choos."

"Not my fault," she chirped brightly. "I'm trying to get you some style, but you refuse to listen to me."

"Mia, I can't do this with you right now. I'm going through some things." A tired note entered her voice. "I just paid your rent, just gave you an allowance. I am not about to give you money for shoes."

Ava had to admit, though, her sister was a bargain hunter. She had a knack for buying designer stuff at unbelievably low prices and dressed like a million bucks. Still, Ava wasn't going to keep supporting her sister's shopping habit.

"I told you I'm paying your money back with my first check."

"How's that going?" Ava asked, changing

27

the subject. Mia had just started working for a studio executive as his personal assistant, or as she preferred to call it, "his concierge."

"It's okay," she whined. "Right now he just has me doing a bunch of menial stuff — running his errands, buying his wife gifts. That's what I'm doing now. I'm in the Hermès store buying her a forty-five-thousand-dollar bag." She sounded tickled by the price. "Can you believe that?"

"Mia, I'm gonna have to call you back."

"What's wrong?" she said, her tone shifting. "You sound down."

Ava let out a long, exasperated sigh. "They're closing my division at the magazine."

"What?" Mia screeched.

At least someone cares, Ava thought. "But the good news is, I'm one of the ones they plan on keeping — if I'm willing to move to another position."

"They offered you another position?" Mia said, her voice perking back up. "Well, if that's the case, then it doesn't sound to me like there's any bad news." She paused. "As long as it's not in Podunk, Idaho, you're cool."

"Mia, it's for the *National Star.*"

Her sister was totally impressed. "The

tabloid rag?"

"Yeah, the tabloid rag."

"Wow, that is so cool." Leave it to her sister, Ava thought darkly, to think chasing after celebrities was cool. "But you know, I can't see you as a tabloid reporter."

"I know. Me either," Ava said.

Mia paused. Ava had told her many times how much integrity in her job meant to her. "Oh well, you'll make it work." Her eternal optimism was kicking back into gear.

"Is that all you have to say?" Ava stared at her degree hanging on the wall. Was this what she went to college for? To chase celebrities and dig up dirt?

"Okay, let's see. What is unemployment paying these days? About four hundred bucks a week, if that? Trust me, I know. Hard choice, though. I can see why you'd have to think about it," Mia sarcastically replied.

"Very funny. Why did I think you would be a voice of reason?"

"I am, dear sister. I think there's no *reason* you should even think of turning this job down."

"Grandma will say I'm selling my soul to the devil," Ava moaned.

"Grandma also says if you cross your eyes, they'll get stuck that way. Give me a break.

29

Girl, you'd better take that job. That stimulus package isn't helping the little people, so folks are still struggling. Besides, how am I supposed to get my Jimmy Choos if you're not working?" she joked.

"You're not getting Jimmy Choos," Ava said. "I —"

"Oh, my God! That's Jada Pinkett Smith!" Mia said, cutting her off. "I gotta go. Everything's gonna work out. Love you. I'll call you back."

As Ava hung up the phone, she couldn't help but smile. Her spoiled little sister worked her nerves, but she always made her feel so much better. Ava knew she had to keep her job not just for herself but for Mia as well. It had been just the two of them against the world for a long time. Their parents and younger brother had died twelve years ago in a car crash. She and Mia had lived with their grandparents since then. But her grandparents were old and Ava had pretty much taken on the maternal role, caring for her little sister. She couldn't stop now.

Ava picked up the contract and grabbed a pen out of her nightstand drawer. She took a deep breath and signed her name. She could only hope this wasn't a decision she would live to regret.

3

The contract was signed, sealed, and tucked away in Ava's briefcase. The agreement was pretty standard, so she wouldn't bother having an attorney review it. Ava would still immediately begin looking for another job. The contract had an "out" clause that allowed her to leave, provided she didn't go work for a competing publication. And since she had no desire to jump to another tabloid rag, that was something she didn't have to worry about.

Ava glanced over at the clock. It was almost ten and Phillip hadn't returned home. She told herself that when he did, she'd apologize. She had been a little harsh, and she would point out how stressful her day had been.

It was nearly eleven when she heard the door open. She debated going down to greet him, but since she was already in bed, reading, she decided to wait until he came up.

Five minutes later, he walked into their bedroom. Ava greeted him with a smile, which quickly disappeared when she saw what was in his hands.

"What are you doing with your suitcases?"

He stared at her, set the luggage on the bed, then walked over to his closet. Ava threw back the covers and climbed out of bed. "Phillip, what's going on?"

He didn't answer as he began putting clothes into his suitcase.

"Are you going somewhere?"

He let out a long sigh, like she was irritating him. "I can't take this, Ava," he finally said. "I'm leaving."

"You can't take what?" she asked, dumbfounded. "And what do you mean, you're leaving?"

He gave her a look of pity. "Ava, who are we kidding? Neither one of us has been happy for a very long time."

"I wonder why." She folded her arms across her chest. She didn't know where all of this was coming from, and Phillip wasn't going anywhere until she got some answers. He was right, she'd been unhappy for a long time, but she hadn't walked out on him. "Is this because I lost my job?" she asked incredulously. That couldn't be it. As much as he had mooched off her, he couldn't be walking out because he thought she'd lost her job.

"This isn't about your job," he said, turning to face her. "It's about you making it seem like I was living off you . . ."

She was about to apologize for saying that when he added, "And it's about me being miserable with you."

Miserable? He was miserable? *She* was the one who came home from a hard day's work every day. *She* was the one receiving harassing letters, and she was the one who stayed horny because he was never "in the mood," and *he* was miserable?

"You have got to be kidding me."

His voice softened. "I'm sorry, Ava. I just can't do it anymore. It . . . it's just that lately . . . I'm discovering some things about myself."

Her eyes widened in surprise. "Come again?" Was he about to tell her he was gay?

"I'm just having some revelations."

"Are you gay?" she bluntly asked.

His mouth opened in shock. "Gay? What? Are you crazy? No, I'm not gay. I just want more than you can give me. Why do you think I haven't married you yet?"

"That's the million-dollar question," Ava said wryly.

"Because I want to marry someone who

wants to be a stay-at-home wife, who enjoys catering to me and my kids and not chasing after some career."

She was outraged by this male chauvinist stunt. "*Somebody* has to chase a career, because you certainly weren't!" She didn't want to go there again, but with this declaration, all bets were off.

"I've been depressed!" he yelled back. "Not that you ever have time to notice! All I do is sit here day in and day out, getting even more depressed about my job, my life. I'm almost thirty-five and I want kids. I want a wife who wants to stay home with her kids."

She was stunned. They had talked about kids, and while Phillip had always bragged that he wanted five or six, she'd never taken him seriously. She might give him two — and *might* was the operative word. And if she did, she definitely wasn't about to stay home with the child.

"The more I thought about the fact that you don't want a lot of children, that you were always so engrossed in your career, the more it bothered me," he continued.

Something still wasn't adding up. "And you didn't see fit to discuss this with me until I announce that I've been laid off?"

"Oh, you'll be fine. I'm sure you'll have

another job by the end of the week. That's just how *driven* you are," he said snidely, like something was wrong with having ambition. "You making me seem trifling just hammered home the fact that you don't even realize what's going on with me."

Ava wanted an answer to her question. "So, if I hadn't told you I lost my job, would you still be leaving me?"

"Sooner or later," he said matter-of-factly as he stuffed more clothes in his suitcase. "This isn't the life I want."

Ava debated discussing their relationship, begging him to give them another chance, but the more she thought about it, the more she knew he was right. He wasn't what she wanted for the rest of her life either, so she shouldn't fight his decision.

Once Ava decided that, she was surprised at how amazingly peaceful she felt. She took a deep breath. "You know what? You're right. We've just been coexisting, so this is probably for the best."

Phillip seemed shocked that she was agreeing with him. He had expected her to be upset, to beg him to change his mind. He was silent for a few moments, then resumed his packing.

Ava numbly made her way downstairs. Even though he was right that they should go their separate ways, she couldn't believe he would choose now to do it. He didn't know that she had another job, so he essentially was kicking her while he thought she was down. That thought filled her with disgust. A real man would never do that. She couldn't wait for him to get out.

Ava blankly watched TV as she waited for him to finish packing. When her cell phone rang and she saw her sister's number, she pressed Ignore. She'd call Mia back after Phillip left. But when the phone rang again and Mia's number popped up, Ava relented.

"Mia, I'm gonna have to call you back."

"Wait!" she said. "I just wanted to let you know I'll be in New York tomorrow. Mr. Abernathy wants me to accompany him there for some business. He's flying back tomorrow night, but I was thinking I could stay over a couple of days and spend time with you."

Ava held the phone tightly. Having Mia here would help her get her mind off the fact that she'd just wasted the last five years. Mia's high spirits would keep her from getting depressed.

"Okay," Ava said. "Your visit couldn't come at a better time."

"You sounded down earlier and you sound even worse now."

"Phillip and I are in the middle of breaking up," Ava whispered.

"Good," Mia proclaimed. "You can do so much better. But I know you're sitting up there all sad, so you're right, this visit was meant to happen!" Her voice became more animated as she went on. "We're flying on his private plane, so we'll get there pretty early. Then I'm free the rest of the day! Stock up the bar — you know I'm legal now. Don't you worry, baby sis is on the way and there will be no pity parties! See ya tomorrow. Smooches!"

Ava smiled as she hung up the phone. Mia really was too much. Her smile faded, though, when she heard Phillip say, "I'll come back for the rest of my things later."

Ava didn't turn around to look at him.

"I'm sorry." He didn't wait for a response as he turned and walked out the door.

She sat in the silence of her living room for a few minutes until she felt a tear trickle down her cheek, which she quickly wiped away. No more of that, she decided. It was a good thing her sister was coming because she didn't want to shed a single tear behind that man she had thought she would marry.

4

Ava was surprised to find out that most of the information found in the *National Star* was based on the truth. That was rule number one, her new boss, Eli, had told her when she handed over the contract to him. *Never just make up stuff.*

"Contrary to popular belief, we don't sit around and create outlandish lies," Eli said. He didn't hide the fact that they would exaggerate at the drop of a dime, but truth always "rested at the core of most of the articles."

Eli went on to clarify that they didn't do "alien gives birth to pigs" stories. That was the *Weekly World Dispatch,* an outrageous tabloid based out of North Carolina. All of the *Star*'s stories were celebrity-driven. But people usually considered the *National Star* guilty by association.

"So, any questions?" Eli asked. He was

sitting at his desk, piled with a stack of papers.

"No, I guess I know all I need to know," she replied.

"And what you don't know, you'll learn."

Eli Lacy was an older man with a head full of white hair, small beady eyes, wrinkled clothes, and an unlit cigarette dangling from his mouth. He was the epitome of what she imagined a tabloid editor would look like.

"Well, duty calls." He handed her a Continental Airlines envelope. "Here's your ticket. Your plane leaves for Aruba in a few hours. You have enough time to get home and pack. And grab your passport. You do have one, don't you?"

She nodded.

"Great, so come back here to meet your photographer no later than one."

"I'm leaving today?" Ava asked. The news had just sunk in. "I can't leave today. My sister just got into town."

"Sorry, darling. You'll have to catch up with your sister next time."

"I can't just leave!" Ava said.

He didn't seem fazed by her outburst. "You can and you will. The wedding is in seven days. We go to press in six. I'd like a blockbuster story by then, please."

Ava could tell by the look on his face that

the issue wasn't open for discussion. Mia was probably already at her house. She was going to be so upset that Ava had to jet out the door.

"Sorry to mess up your plans, but you know how this game works. Plus, you're a pro, so you can handle it," Eli said as he handed her another envelope. "The reporter that was going to cover the story got the freaking swine flu! So we had to bring in someone experienced because there's a major scandal brewing with Miss Wright. And you're our girl." He was talking so fast, Ava could barely keep up. "Now, that envelope I just gave you contains more information on India, as well as info on one of our contacts, Juliette Carlone. She's a seamstress and her daughter was married to Fredericko, our loving beau, at one point. Don't know if you can get her to talk, but you need to interview her first." He waved his hand slightly. "You also have some cash in there in case you have to pay anyone off. Your photographer will know how to go about getting more money if you need it. You'll also find in there a MasterCard for your expenses, along with a sheet detailing the company's policies regarding the use of the card."

Ava was stunned. During all the time

she'd been with *Newswire,* she had never been given a credit card. She had to pay all of her expenses and wait to be reimbursed.

He pointed at her. "Our sources are confident that this story is real. So bring back a doozy. I had my secretary call a car service to take you home so you can get packed. They'll wait, then bring you back here to meet your photographer. Any questions?"

"No, I guess," she said slowly, trying to process everything.

"Great," Eli said crisply. The fact that he picked up his phone and began dialing told Ava that she was dismissed.

Ava was still in a state of confusion as the driver took her back to her brownstone. Everything was going at supersonic speed. Not only did she have a new job but within hours of showing up the first day, she was heading out of town to cover what could be the biggest scandal of the year.

As soon as Ava pushed the front door open, her sister sprang from her seat on the sofa. "Hey, big sis!" she said, racing over and throwing her arms around her sister's neck. She'd been able to let herself in because she still had a key from the two months she'd lived with Ava right after graduating from the University of Arkansas.

That hadn't worked out too well, Ava remembered. As relaxed as she tried to be, she couldn't take her sister staying out until all hours of the night. So when a temporary assistant job had opened up in Los Angeles, Mia had jumped at the chance to "get out from under Ava's wing."

"Hey, little sis," Ava said, feeling her sister's love radiating from her.

"What are you doing home so early?" Mia asked as she walked back over to the sofa. "I thought you said you wouldn't be home until around six. How's the new job?"

Ava dropped her purse. "Bad news. My new job is sending me to Aruba."

"Aruba?" Mia marveled. "How totally cool is that. And for what?"

"A story. And they're sending me today." Ava glanced at her watch. "In, like, a couple of hours."

Mia stuck her bottom lip out. "Aww, man. I wanted us to hang."

"I know." Ava sighed. "I'm so sorry. You know you're welcome to hang out here until you have to go back." She looked around the apartment. At least the laptop was gone from the couch. "Phillip moved out. I'll have to fill you in on that later. I'm not in the mood to talk about that now."

Mia nodded in understanding. "I guess I

will chill here. I need to catch up on my sleep anyway, and my girlfriend from school, Tammy, is here, so maybe I can hang out with her."

Ava was glad her sister wasn't throwing a temper tantrum, which wouldn't have been out of character for her.

"Well, come talk to me while I pack," Ava said. Mia followed her upstairs and lay across the bed while Ava pulled out her suitcases.

"So, you didn't tell me what you're going to Aruba for," Mia said.

"Chasing celebrity dirt." Ava pulled her underwear out of her top drawer and dropped several pairs into her suitcase.

"Ooooh, anyone I know?"

Ava pulled open the drawer she kept her nightclothes in. "Only if you know India Wright."

"Aaaah!" Mia squealed as she jumped off the bed. "You're going to do a story on India Wright? *The* India Wright?" She started fanning herself in excitement. "Oh, my God! Oh, my God! I, like, so absolutely love her! It's my dream to be her personal assistant!"

Ava looked at her sister with hooded eyes. "Give me a break."

"No, seriously!" She grabbed her sister's

arm. "Oh, my God. Please let me come with you, please, please, please!"

Ava jerked her arm away. "You've got to be kidding me!"

"No, I'm not. That would be my greatest dream in life. If I meet India, show her what I can do, I know she'd hire me."

"Number one," Ava said sternly, "I'm not taking my kid sister with me on the first assignment for my new job. Number two, I'm a professional. How would it look to have my little sister harassing a celebrity for a job?"

"I wouldn't harass her. I would just slide her my résumé," Mia said, striking a pose, "then dazzle her with my personality. She'd be begging you to get me to come work for her."

Ava wasn't giving her sister any encouragement. "Not. Going. To. Happen." She walked into her closet. "Besides, don't you have to get back to work? I'll tell you all the details when I get back. And I'll make sure to take plenty of pictures."

"Ugggh! I wish you'd quit treating me like a child!" Mia stomped out of the room and down the stairs.

Ava couldn't help but smile. There went her sister's temper tantrum. *I wasn't thinking clearly,* it occurred to her, *or I would've never mentioned India.*

Twenty minutes later, Ava was packed and back downstairs, facing her sister. She'd called the car service to let them know she was on her way back out.

"I have to go," Ava said, picking up her purse and the envelope with her itinerary off the coffee table. "Are you sure you're going to be okay?"

Mia sat on the sofa, her arms folded across her chest, her lips stuck out, pouting. "You sure you don't want to call a babysitter to watch me while I'm here?"

Ava laughed as she leaned over and lightly kissed her sister on the head. "Bye, spoiled brat. I love you, make yourself at home. Sorry I don't have a chance to spend time with you, but I'll make a special trip to L.A. so we can spend a weekend together."

"Fine," Mia said, not taking her eyes off the TV. "Oh, and I love you, too."

Ava was closing the door when she heard her sister add, "But I'm still mad!"

Forty-five minutes later, Ava was back at the *Star* headquarters, struggling to pull her suitcases across the wide sidewalk. The driver had left her at the curb because she hadn't thought to ask where she was meeting her photographer. Now she had to lug her suitcases inside to find out where she was supposed to be going.

"You need some help with that?"

Ava turned to see Clifton, the man she'd met yesterday. Seeing her frown, he immediately jumped on the defensive. "I know you can handle stuff yourself, but my mother didn't raise me to ignore a woman struggling with her luggage."

Ava managed a smile as she stepped back. "Cliff, right?" He nodded. "Be my guest." She pointed to the suitcase.

Cliff eyed her skeptically, then eased over to pick up the luggage.

"Dang, we're only going for a week," he said as he tried to lift the second suitcase, wobbling on its wheels.

Ava's eyebrows shot up. "We?"

He adjusted the suitcase handles, then turned to her. "Yes, we. I'm your photographer." He quickly added, "I guess they didn't tell you. But don't worry, I'll stay out of your way." It was obvious he was still gun-shy from the way she'd treated him the other day.

Oh, great, Ava thought. Her very first tabloid assignment and her photographer was a man she'd rubbed the wrong way.

He cocked his head, pointing. "Well, let's go. I'm taking the company truck to the airport. It's parked this way." He didn't wait on her as he wheeled both suitcases toward the parking garage.

Ava quickly followed after him.

They didn't say much on the ride to the airport. She tried to make small talk, but he answered in monosyllables and didn't initiate any conversation.

After they were checked in for their international flight, Ava took a seat next to Cliff in the gate waiting area.

"Ummm, would you like some coffee?" she asked after a minute of silence. "I'm about to make a Starbucks run."

"Nah, I'm good," he said, not bothering to look up from his *Sports Illustrated* magazine.

Ava sighed. "Look, it's going to be a long week. We have to work together, so we're going to need to talk."

He slowly raised his head and eyed her skeptically.

She smiled and stuck out her hand. "I'm sorry. I know I might've come off the wrong way on our first meeting."

"Might have?" he asked, but without any edge to his voice.

She gave him a half smile. "Okay, so I did come off the wrong way. But I was having a really bad day. Can we start over? I'm having a hard enough time adjusting to this new job as it is. The last thing I need to be doing is going to a foreign country, fighting with the one person I'm working with."

He closed his magazine and studied her. "Okay," he said. "Let's start over. After all, we're about to head to a beautiful island, and while it's work, I'd like to think we can be friends and enjoy a little play, too."

Ava didn't know whether he was flirting with her or what. It had been so long since she'd wanted a man to show interest that she couldn't really tell.

She decided not to read anything into his comment, and also decided not to get coffee. She wanted to build on their new rapport.

"So, do you like working for the *Star*?" she asked, trying not to gaze too deeply into his enchanting brown eyes. She was just now realizing how gorgeous they were.

"It's okay," he said. "But only because all I do is take the photos, and I love doing that." He looked around to make sure no one was listening before leaning in. "I have a collection of photos of celebrities out of their element, you know, doing normal stuff. Some without makeup, spending time with their kids, their pets. It's really eye-opening. When I complete it, it will be an exhibit called Unmasked."

"Wow," she said, intrigued. She could feel the passion in his words. "I'm surprised they let you take those."

"Well, that's where the tabloid part comes in," he admitted. "Most don't know I took them. But when I'm finished, I won't use a photo of anyone who doesn't give permission. I just think that while they wouldn't agree to it up front, when they see the finished product, they'll fall in love with it."

"Wow, again," she said. "I can't wait to see it."

He looked around again. "You don't have to wait." He popped open his laptop. They waited for the computer to boot up, then Cliff clicked on a slideshow.

"Oh my, those are phenomenal," she said, watching one picture after another. By the time they'd reached the last slide, she was in awe. "Yeah, I can't see anyone saying no to that. They may be mad for a minute that you took a picture without their knowledge, but when they see how they turned out . . ."

He closed the laptop. "I hope so. And I'm not even done yet."

Ava leaned back, moved not only by the quality of the photos he'd shared with her but by the connection she felt when he talked about his work. Add to that the fact that he was so attractive, with his masculine

49

features and strong physique, and Ava had to quickly regain her composure. Because the one lesson she had learned over all these years of working was that business and pleasure never mixed.

Yet she couldn't deny the delicious tingle of being attracted to a new man. The more she thought about it, the more Ava knew she wanted some pleasure on this trip. She *needed* some pleasure. At this point, she almost felt like her sanity depended on it.

5

Ava was in awe. The five-star hotel looked like it had jumped right off the pages of a travel brochure. She grinned from ear to ear as the taxi driver unloaded their luggage.

Cliff paid the driver, then the two of them made their way through the revolving doors and over to the check-in counter. Cliff went to one clerk while Ava walked over to another.

"Hi, checking in for Ava Cole." She slid her driver's license to the clerk, who took it and began tapping his keyboard. Ava had just pulled out the credit card when the clerk said, "Oh, Miss Cole, everything is already covered. Your room and tax, as well as your incidentals."

The woman handed her the room key. "Enjoy your stay."

Ava looked over at Cliff and smiled. She could get used to this royal treatment.

"I thought you knew," he said. "Membership does have its privileges."

She laughed and was walking away from the counter when a large crowd came bustling in the door. The group had to be at least twenty people. Ava immediately recognized India Wright. Several patrons recognized her, too, because the lobby started buzzing. A few people whipped out their cell phones to get India's picture. She smiled politely, but a huge, burly man who had to be a bodyguard, kept people from getting too close. A handsome, olive-skinned man walked beside India, and Ava recognized Fredericko from his pictures. He looked even better in person. He gazed all around, smiling for the cameras as if he were the star.

With the exception of a nerd wearing a suit, everyone else was dressed casually, including one of the sexiest men Ava had ever seen. The sight of him stopped her in her tracks. He was about six-four, two hundred pounds, with strong chiseled features, wavy hair, and a body that made her heart beat a little faster.

A woman in her midtwenties approached the counter. "Hi, I'm Jackie Baptiste. We have reservations for India Wright. Eight rooms and the penthouse suite."

The clerk flashed a huge smile. "Yes, Miss Baptiste, everything has been taken care of. And Miss Wright's room is awaiting her arrival." The clerk slid an envelope toward Jackie. "You'll find all of the room keys in here." She handed her another envelope. "This one is for Miss Wright's room. As requested, she is in our private penthouse suite and everyone else is on the twelfth floor. Please let us know if we can do anything else for you."

Ava caught the eye of the handsome man and wanted to melt when he flashed a sideways smile at her as he followed India to the elevator.

"So, are you gonna make a move right now?" Cliff asked, breaking her out of her trance. "And I don't mean on that man you're breathing so heavy at."

"Was it that obvious?" she said.

He nodded. "It was."

"Well, no, I'm going to give her time to get settled in. Eli said he'll let me know what time my interview with her is."

"Cool. I'm going to go up and get settled in myself. We'll hook back up in, say, an hour?"

They both headed up in the elevator. Once inside her room, Ava found it had a beautiful oceanside view. The room was just as nice as the rest of the hotel. It was filled with contemporary furniture, and the plush white bedding was beckoning. Ava slid open the balcony door and stepped outside. She smiled at the sight of the white sandy beach and turquoise waters. The beach below was lined with lovers taking evening strolls. It was absolutely gorgeous, and for a minute, Ava wished she were in Aruba on her honeymoon with Phillip, not chasing some story.

"Looks like that will never happen," she mumbled as she made her way back inside the spacious hotel room. She unpacked, hanging her clothes up in the closet, then stretched out across the luxurious bed.

"This is the life! I could so get used to this!" Ava sang. She lay across the bed for a few minutes, then decided she'd better call Eli to let him know she'd arrived.

"Yes, I'd like to place a call and bill it to my credit card," Ava told the operator after she'd dialed the number. She ran the MasterCard the company had given her lightly through her fingers. The company policy sheet had said that this card was to be used at her disposal to get her story.

Ava gave the operator her card number, then waited for Eli to pick up.

"Hey," she said, after he answered. "I'm

here, checked in and ready to work."

"Good," Eli replied. He was a no-nonsense type of guy who obviously took his job very seriously, since it was after ten in New York and he was still at the office. Ava could picture his bushy eyebrows scrunched up as he talked. He didn't ask anything about her flight or hotel, just cut straight to business. "Have you seen India?"

"Yeah, I saw her and Fredericko in the lobby when I was checking in. I tried to —"

"Good," Eli said, cutting her off. "So you have the file on India and Fredericko. That should give you all the background you need. We confirmed your interview time with India. It's set up for nine in the morning. You'll have fifteen minutes with her."

"What?" Ava bolted upright. "Fifteen minutes? Are you serious?"

"As triple-bypass surgery," he said, a lame attempt at humor.

"How in the world am I supposed to do a full-length cover story in fifteen minutes?"

He laughed, delighted by her naïveté. "Because the real story will be in what she doesn't tell you."

Ava let out a small groan.

"Look." He sighed, sensing her reservations. "You can do this. Just hunt down the story behind the story. Nobody cares about the inspiration for her last album, or how she finally found true love. We want the nit and grit."

A bad taste was filling her mouth. "What is that supposed to mean?"

"I told you, Miss India Wright is hiding something and I want to know what it is. Dig up some dirt because I need a bombshell. Every media outlet in town is covering that story and I need to stand out. While everyone else is reporting on the fabulous nuptials, I want you to bring me something no one else has, a story that will have everyone talking. Find out what India is hiding."

"Like she's going to tell me."

His voice became harder. "You're a reporter, report. Now, if you need more cash, just get with Cliff. He has the info for us to wire whatever you need."

Ava had been too stunned to process everything when she'd first gotten the cash, so she asked what she'd been wondering from the start. "What would I need cash for?"

Eli laughed. "Darling, shed the journalistic standards. Here at the *Star* we get the story by any means necessary, and sometimes that requires a buttload of cash."

Cash for stories? Ava's stomach churned

at the idea.

"So get to it," Eli continued. "Call me when you have something."

Eli didn't give her a chance to respond before he hung up the phone.

6

The sun tickled Ava out of her sleep. Blazing tropical light was peering in through the open silk curtains. Ava and Cliff had hung out by the bar last night, trading journalistic war stories. At first, their camaraderie seemed a little stiff, but after a couple of drinks, they both relaxed. Cliff had a great sense of humor, she'd discovered, and he was so easy to talk to. It had felt good to have a decent conversation with a man. Before the night was over, Ava found herself telling Cliff all about the threatening letters. He made her promise to report them when she returned home to New York, and he even offered to go with her to the nearest precinct house.

Ava stretched and pulled herself out of bed. She walked over to the large bay window and looked outside. The gorgeous seascape actually made her heart ache. This was a sight she should be sharing with someone she loved.

Ava was jolted out of her thoughts by a knock on her hotel door. She glanced at the clock on the nightstand. It couldn't be anyone but Cliff, but they weren't supposed to meet for another two hours.

"Who is it?" she asked, walking toward the door.

"Room service," the voice called out.

Ava peered through the peephole. She spied a man dressed in a waiter's uniform, with a large rolling tray parked next to him.

"I didn't order room service," she replied. Working in news had made Ava more than a little paranoid. She didn't think whoever was sending her those threatening letters would follow her to the Caribbean, but she couldn't be too careful.

The waiter checked a note in his hands. "This is compliments of Miss India Wright."

Ava hesitated. India was sending her room service? "Okay, fine. Just leave the tray."

The waiter looked momentarily agitated, but did as he was told. Ava waited until she could no longer see him out of the peephole before she stuck her head out the door, then grabbed the tray and rolled it inside.

"What the . . . ?" she mumbled when she took the top off the silver platter. It held enough food to feed five people. She scoped out the scrambled eggs; crisp, hickory-smoked, streaky bacon; hash browns; grilled organic tomatoes and sautéed potatoes; as well as French toast. She picked up the note: *Looking forward to a dynamic interview. Smooches, India.*

Ava laughed as she tossed the note down. So India was one of those stars who tried to make nice with the journalists prior to the interview? Ava poured a cup of coffee, then wheeled the tray out on the balcony. Who was she to complain about the deluxe treatment?

So this is what it feels like to be a star, she thought as she plopped down in the plush chaise longue on the balcony.

Ava soon finished her breakfast, or at least as much of it as she could eat. She wanted to take a look around the massive twenty-four-acre property before her interview. She went through her morning ritual, then changed into some comfortable business attire before making her way downstairs to the bar.

"Can I get a glass of orange juice?" she asked the bartender. She really wasn't thirsty, but she just wanted to kill some time by sitting around, taking in the ambience.

"I know it's early, but this is Aruba," the bartender said with a sexy Latin accent.

"How about a mimosa?"

"No, thank you. I'm on duty right now, but you can believe I'll be back before the night is over." She winked at him.

"I'll be waiting right here," he said, setting a glass down in front of her, then filling it with orange juice. "This is on me."

Ava thanked him, then turned away with a coy look. Being single again was fun.

"Ah, drinking on the job?"

Ava looked up to see a man she recognized as the incredibly handsome one who had checked in with India. Today he was wearing a white silk shirt — open enough to give a peek of his bare chest — navy slacks, and Italian loafers. He gently licked his lips, then flashed a sinfully bright smile, a smile that made her insides flip.

"Nonalcoholic," she said, holding up her drink. "And how do you know I'm on the job?"

"I make it my business to know everything about my client and whom she deals with, Miss Cole." He extended a manicured hand. "Julian Lowe," he said. "I'm India's manager."

"Hi, Julian Lowe." He must really have been on top of things to know who she was, considering she'd just been given this assignment two days ago.

61

"Are you all set for your interview? Is there anything I can get for you?" Julian asked.

"No, I'm fine. Looking forward to chatting with India." She motioned around the hotel lobby, which was already bustling with people. "I'm just soaking in the atmosphere until it's my time."

"Yes, India is up now with a reporter from *People* magazine." He stopped and considered her, obviously weighing his words carefully. "I hope you don't take offense," he said. "But can you tell me what a beautiful, seemingly intelligent woman like you is doing working for the *National Star*?"

Ava struggled to contain her groan. The last thing she wanted was for word to get around that she was bad-mouthing her employer. "It's a job." She shrugged. "And in these tough times you have to take what you can get."

He leaned in closer. "Do you mind if I ask why you left *Newswire* magazine?"

Wow, he really has done his homework. "They shut down our division, and, well, here I am."

His piercing gaze gave her goose bumps. "Well, I hope it's only temporary. A stepping-stone to bigger and better things."

They were standing quite close, and she

62

could feel the chemistry between them. Ava was very attracted to Julian. She didn't know if it was because she had been so sexually frustrated with Phillip or because Julian was so sexy. Either way, she was having fantasies that had nothing to do with work.

"So, tell me," Julian said, breaking the silence, "are you here by yourself? I mean, besides your colleague, the photographer."

She smiled. "Yes, this trip is purely work."

He shook his head slightly. "I know you're here to cover the wedding, but you didn't bring anyone to enjoy this beautiful country with? Even with work, this is not a place where a beautiful woman like yourself should be alone." He didn't try to hide the fact that he was flirting, and Ava was loving every minute of it.

"No. I'm on my own. What about yourself?"

He made a comic face of despair. "India is usually more than enough for me to handle. But she is spending more and more time with her fiancé, and I'm finding myself with nothing to do. So maybe, Miss Cole, you will allow me to take you to dinner."

Ava intended to say no, but her mouth wouldn't let her. Instead she said, "I'd like that."

His expression relayed his pleasure. "Great. We'll meet in the lobby. Let's say seven?"

She nodded. "Seven sounds good."

"Good luck with your interview. I have to go meet with someone from the record label or else I'd sit in." He gently took her hand and kissed it. "But for now, *adiós, mi* sweet *amiga. Me muero ganas de conocerte.*"

Ava had no idea what he had just said, but it sounded so sexy that it sent a tingling sensation through her body.

7

Images of Julian were still fresh in her mind as Ava moved to the lobby, still killing time. She'd decided to hang downstairs and people watch until her interview. Tanned couples floated past her, heading out to shop. Others were filing out onto the back patio, ready for a day on the beach.

"Mind if I join you?"

Ava looked up to see Cliff standing over her table.

"Hey, you." She glanced at her watch. "You're a little early, aren't you?"

He pulled out a chair. "I came downstairs for probably the same reason you did, to take in the sights."

Ava smiled slyly. "Umm-hmm. You came to watch the pretty women strolling by in their skimpy bikinis."

Cliff returned her smile. "I'm sitting across from a pretty woman, so why would I need to look somewhere else?"

He was flirting, too? Ava could get used to this. Cliff didn't have the smooth eloquence Julian did, but he was a fine-looking man.

Business and pleasure don't mix, she quickly reminded herself. She was just about to say something when the sight of a tall, model-looking beauty sashaying through the revolving doors of the hotel stopped her short. The young woman wore huge sunglasses and a floppy-brimmed white hat, along with a flowing white sundress. Although she looked like a celebrity, her appearance wiped the smile right off Ava's face.

She jumped up from the table. "Mia Dawn Cole! What in the world are you doing?" Ava called out, stomping over to her sister.

"Sissy!" Mia exclaimed, thrilled by her surroundings.

"Don't 'sissy' me!" Ava said. "What the hell are you doing in Aruba?"

"I'm vacationing," she sang.

"Since when?" Ava sternly said.

Mia cocked her finger at her. "Since my sister up and decided to come hang out with the hottest star in the country and tried to leave me alone in her apartment."

"I am not hanging out with India! I'm

working."

Mia waved her off. "Please." She looked around the lavish hotel. "If you're working, this is the kind of job I need to have."

Ava was not about to be put off. "Mia, answer me. Why are you here? How did you get here? A last-minute ticket to Aruba had to cost an arm and a leg."

"Umm, I do work, you know," she said, like she was offended.

"Mia . . ."

She broke out in a huge grin as she reached in her purse and pulled out a credit card. "Okay, okay. I used Mr. Abernathy's American Express Black card." She wiggled it a little. "I booked my flight, paid for my room here. Oh yes, you don't have to worry. I got my own room because I figured one of us might meet someone and need to get our freak on. But I did have them put me in the room next to you. I even paid for my driver."

"What? Have you lost your mind? You used your boss's card?"

"The man is a billionaire." Mia shrugged. "This is nothing. Do you know he sent his daughter and ten of her friends to Paris last month for her eighteenth birthday? Anyway" — she pulled a BlackBerry out of her purse and flashed it at her sister — "his only requirement was that I keep my company

67

phone close by." She shook her head as she dropped the phone back in her purse. "Why he has to have a special phone to call is beyond me. Now I have to lug around two phones. But that's how rich, eccentric people are. So don't feel sorry for him."

Ava stared at her sister in disbelief. She knew Mia could be flighty at times and even irresponsible, but this took the cake.

"I cannot believe you stole the man's credit card to come here!"

Mia pulled back. "What? Stole? I didn't steal anything. This is my card. Well," she amended, "it's in Mr. Abernathy's name, but I'm an authorized user. I am his personal concierge, remember?"

Ava wasn't buying that excuse. "Mia, I don't think the man gave you a credit card to go off on personal trips with. So you sneaking his card to buy a plane ticket amounts to stealing."

She let out a long huff. "As usual, you think the worst of me. I tell you, he gave me permission to buy the ticket, pay for the room, and everything else." She shook her head like she couldn't believe her sister would doubt her. "I'm insulted, and hurt."

Ava looked momentarily apologetic. "Wow, I'm sorry. That . . . that's just hard to imagine. I mean, he let you use his card?"

Mia dropped the card back into her bag and winked. "He didn't want me to miss my grandma's funeral."

Ava rolled her eyes. "I should've known. Mia, how many times are you gonna kill off Grandma? Would you just let her rest in peace?" Their paternal grandmother had died of a heart attack eight years ago, and anytime Mia wanted to get out of something, she killed the poor woman all over again.

Mia ignored her sister as she removed her sunglasses. "Well, well, well, what have we here?" she said, glancing over Ava's shoulder.

Ava turned to see Cliff had come up behind her.

"Hey, um, Ava, I just wanted to make sure you were all right."

"Hello, I'm Mia." She stepped toward Cliff and extended her hand. "And aren't you the new Calvin Klein model?"

Ava rolled her eyes. "Oh, good grief." Her sister was always flirtatious.

Cliff blushed like a teenager. The whole scene was nauseating.

"Mia, this is Cliff, my photographer. Cliff, this is my hardheaded sister, Mia."

Mia ignored the dig as she let her hand linger in his. "Now I see why you didn't want me to come," she said, leaning back and looking at Cliff's behind.

"Mia, please," Ava said, pulling her sister's hand away.

"Ava, you didn't tell me you were having your sister meet you here," Cliff said, finally speaking up. Ava didn't like how he seemed infatuated with her sister.

"That's because I didn't want her here." She turned to Mia. "How did you know what hotel I was staying at, anyway?"

"I saw your itinerary when you went to go pack," Mia informed her. "Did you really think I was going to let you get this close to India Wright and I not tag along?" She slid her glasses back on her face. "I don't think so."

Ava sighed in frustration as she looked down at her watch. It was time for them to get upstairs for the interview. She'd have to deal with her sister later. "This is not over, missy."

"I'm going to get settled in," Mia sang. "You go do your work and we'll hook up later." She flashed a sexy smile at Cliff. "Or *we* can hook up later." She quickly looked at her sister and said, "Unless of course you want him."

Ava couldn't believe her sister had put her on the spot like that. "No, I don't want him." Cliff looked insulted, and Ava touched his arm. "I didn't mean it like that," she said quickly, correcting herself. "I mean, he's a work colleague. But he's still off-limits for you."

"We'll let Cliffy decide about that," Mia said. "Catch up with you later! Smooches." She waved at her sister as she sashayed toward the front desk.

"Cliff! His name is Cliff," Ava called out after her sister. She shook her head in exasperation as she noticed Cliff watching her sister's backside with a grin on his face.

"Excuse me?" It was her turn to be insulted.

Cliff caught himself and turned his attention back to Ava. "What did I do? She's cute."

Ava gave him the evil eye.

He chuckled. "Rest easy. Not my type. But she's still cute." He playfully pinched her chin. "But what does it matter? It's not like you want me anyway. I'm just a work colleague."

"Shut up and let's go," Ava said, heading toward the elevator. That's all she needed. Her sister had blown into town like a tornado, and Ava had a feeling this trip was about to be a whole lot more drama than she'd expected.

8

You have to be kidding me. That's all Ava could think as she sat across from India, who had plastered on a fake smile and was talking about how much her music meant to her.

". . . and without my music, I'd simply be lost," India continued as she crossed her legs and dangled her foot. She had on the baddest pair of Gucci pumps Ava had ever seen. India looked every bit the diva darling the media portrayed her to be. Of course, her makeup was flawless and she wore a slinky white sequined top that was the perfect mix of professional and casual. The tee and her black leggings accentuated her perfect figure, and her long honey brown curls cascaded down her back.

Ava glanced down at her Sony digital recorder. She'd been recording for eight minutes. Eight of the longest, most boring minutes of her life. India had such personality on the stage and screen, but she sucked in her interview. Cliff had snapped a few action photos and was now sitting off to the side looking bored as well.

Ava decided to take charge of the conversation. She didn't know Eli that well, but she knew this interview wouldn't cut it with him. There was no way it would move any magazines.

"So, tell me about Fredericko; where'd you two meet?" Ava asked.

India's smile quickly faded and she looked like she didn't want to answer.

"Surely you knew I'd ask about your impending nuptials," Ava said, lifting an eyebrow.

"Well, yes, of course," India said, trying to appear comfortable again. "I just thought your readers would want to know more about my passion for music."

You thought wrong, Ava wanted to say. The *National Star* didn't move 1.5 million units a week because they regurgitated press releases and bios.

"We'll be sure to include all of that, but what the people really want to know is about Fredericko," Ava said. "How did you two meet? What made you know he was the one? That sort of thing."

"Umm, well, we met when I was visiting

Aruba a year ago . . . and let's just say it was love at first sight." There went that fake smile again. Ava's antenna immediately went up. She asked a few more questions, and had she been reporting in her old job, she'd have left it at that and not gone on a digging expedition through India's personal life. But since she was on the tabloid-side of journalism now, she knew she needed to dredge deeper for the scandal that seemed to be brewing beneath India's story.

"Is it true that Fredericko doesn't work? And that you're not making him sign a prenup?" Ava felt sleazy asking that question, but since Eli had pointed out both of those issues, she knew she couldn't leave without asking India to address them.

"I beg your pardon?" India asked, losing her smile.

"I don't mean to get personal, but these are the questions that our readers want answered."

India gritted her teeth, obviously trying to not get an attitude. "I'm sure that your readers would much rather know about my music."

Yeah right. Ava wanted to snicker. "Miss Wright, I assure you, our readers are much more interested in your personal life than your professional life."

74

India rolled her eyes. "My personal life is no one's business. You know I'm getting married. You know I'm happy. That's all that should matter." She flashed her fake smile again. "So —"

"*Forbes* says you're one of the highest-paid female entertainers out there. Why wouldn't you have a prenup?" Ava pressed, interrupting India.

India glared at her, but Ava didn't back down. "That information was widely reported by the *New York Daily News*," Ava said. "Didn't your handlers advise you that it would be wise to have a prenup, especially when you're about to marry a man who is unemployed?"

India abruptly stood up and motioned toward her assistant, Jackie Baptiste. She had showed Ava in and remained hovering in the corner during the entire interview. As soon as India summoned her, she seemed to magically appear at her side. "Jackie, isn't it time to wrap this up?"

"But I'm not finished," Ava said, standing as well.

India tried her best to compose herself, but her anger was evident. "Oh, but you are," she snapped. "Jackie, get me the damn publicist and find out why we're talking to a freakin' tabloid magazine in the first place."

She stormed out of the sitting area and into her bedroom. The door slammed so hard it made Ava jump.

Jackie marched over and stood in front of Ava. She folded her arms across her chest. "You and your photographer can show yourselves out, please."

Ava sighed as she submitted to her fate. Something had told her that this interview wouldn't go well, but she definitely hadn't thought it would be this bad. Now what was she supposed to do?

Eli's words came back to her: "India Wright is hiding something and I want to know what it is. Dig up some dirt because I need a bombshell."

9

As soon as the elevator doors closed, Cliff shook his head. "I know you may be a talented journalist, but I don't know how you're going to pull a decent story out of that. That interview was so boring, I could barely stay awake. Well, except for the end, when I thought she was going to slug you," he joked.

"She did look like she wanted to slap me silly, didn't she?" Ava laughed before turning solemn again. "I hate getting down in the gutter," she told him, "but how else am I going to get the story that Eli wants?"

"Well, you're not going to get it from her, that's for sure." Cliff glanced down and started toying with the display screen on the back of his camera. "Look at that one," he said, holding the camera out to reveal a candid shot of India in midlaugh. The star looked like she was made to be in front of a camera.

"That's hot," Ava replied in admiration. "You are really good. Are you going to add any of these to your exhibit?"

Cliff continued clicking through images. "Nah, they're not candid enough, but hopefully I'll get some before the week is out." He snapped the camera off, and with a professional's ease, he slipped it into a pocket in his bag. "At least you'll have some awesome photos. Don't know how you're going to get a good story to go along with it."

Ava murmured in agreement. "I don't know much about Eli, but I can tell that what I have isn't going to fly."

As they stepped off the elevator, Cliff nodded. "I do know a lot about Eli and I can tell you it definitely won't fly."

The two of them crossed the sumptuous lobby, and Cliff gestured toward the bright outdoors. "I can't wait to see the island. How about we knock out this interview with the seamstress, grab something to eat, and then go sightseeing?"

Ava broke out in a huge grin. "Depends on how the day goes. I have dinner plans."

Cliff raised an eyebrow. "What? We just got here. You're picking up men already?"

She turned her nose up, not appreciating the accusatory look that crossed his face.

78

"Excuse me?"

Cliff kept his voice neutral. "I'm just saying, we haven't been in Aruba twenty-four hours and you already have a date? Is it someone you met here?"

"Well, that's really none of your business. If we're not working, then it seems like who I eat with isn't your concern."

Cliff held his hands up. "Whoa, back up. I'm sorry. I didn't mean it like that." He sighed heavily as they continued down around the hotel driveway. Beyond, the ocean crests were flashing in the sun. "It seems like I'm always rubbing you the wrong way."

"Yeah, it seems that way."

"Well, I was just asking."

"It's the way you asked," Ava snapped.

"I'm sorry, it's just that we're in a strange country. You know what happened to that girl from Alabama?"

Ava rolled her eyes. Her grandmother had brought up Natalee Holloway, too, when Ava called her. But she wasn't a teenager, and she wasn't going to disappear.

"It's not like I picked up some stranger in the street. If you must know, I'm having dinner with Julian Lowe, India's manager." Ava couldn't help but smile brightly at the mention of Julian. Just saying his name set off butterflies in her stomach.

"Oh," he said, as though he didn't quite know how to process that. "Well, maybe you can pick him for some information." An interested look crossed his face. "Maybe that's why you're going out with him in the first place. Girl, you have this tabloid reporting thing down after all."

She turned her nose up, offended. "I'll have you know that I'm not using Julian to dig up dirt on India. I'm going to dinner because he asked me to go to dinner. And I have no intention of using him to get a story."

Cliff shrugged off her comment. "Whatever you say. But you might want to think about getting whatever you can from him. Because that," he said, pointing to the digital recorder clutched in her hand, "isn't worth squat."

"Tell me about it." She sighed and went back to wondering what in the world she was going to do about this story. She just hoped the seamstress would give her enough to work with.

"So, you ready to go talk to" — she pulled a piece of paper out of her purse — "Juliette Carlone? Her shop is right down this street."

Cliff eyed her sideways, and if she didn't know any better, she'd think he was mad at her. "Whatever."

"Cliff, do you have an attitude with me?"

He forced a smile as he reached over and playfully hugged her. "I'm just giving you a hard time."

She could tell by the tone of his voice that he was serious, and she was actually shocked that she had a tingling feeling inside. How long had it been since someone had been jealous over her? And she could tell Cliff was definitely jealous. Ava couldn't help but like how it made her feel. Phillip never noticed if she was still alive.

She shook off the thought. You'd better watch out, she told herself. She'd barely broken up with her fiancé and was already attracted to two different men.

Ava snuck one last glance at Cliff as they reached the shop door. She motioned toward the store's sign. "Let's go get our story."

10

Ava slowly opened the door to the shop. A soft chime signaled their arrival. The interior was lit by sunshine flooding in through windows with the shutters folded back. An elderly lady sitting behind an old sewing machine looked up at them. Her face bore the deep lines of someone who had seen the worst that life had to offer. Her eyes were droopy and weary. Depression was written all over her face.

"Yes?"

Ava looked at Cliff, and he nodded his support. She walked over to the woman. "Hi, my name is Ava Cole and this is my photographer, Cliff. We're from the *National Star*. We were told it was okay to come talk to you."

The woman eyed them pensively, and Ava quickly continued. "We won't take up much of your time, I promise. We just need some information about Fredericko de la Cruz."

At the mention of Fredericko's name, the woman's entire demeanor changed. Her body tensed as a look of hatred blanketed her face. She began uttering a string of what had to be unflattering terms in her native tongue.

"Well, we were just wondering if you could help us," Ava said, cutting off the woman's ranting.

The woman glared at Ava like she was studying her, seemingly unsure how, or if, she should respond. Finally she looked over at Cliff. "He's with you?"

Ava nodded. "Yes, he's my photographer."

"Lock my door," the woman said to him.

Cliff hurried over and locked her door, and then both he and Ava took a seat in the two chairs in front of the sewing machine.

"What would you like to know about that scoundrel?"

Those were fighting words, Ava thought. "We're just wondering if you can tell us a little about him, his background, his relationship with your daughter."

The woman took a deep breath to calm herself. "As you can see, I don't think too fondly of Fredericko," she said with disdain.

"Why is that?" Ava asked, easing out her digital tape recorder. She was worried that the woman would clam up when she saw the recorder, but she didn't pay it any attention.

"My daughter, God rest her soul, she gives her heart to that snake and he swallows it up whole," the woman said, spitting like the mere mention of Fredericko hurt her tongue.

Ava glanced at Cliff. She hoped this woman was legit, because she definitely had no problem giving Ava all the information she wanted.

"So he dated your daughter?" Ava pressed.

"Dated? He was married to her. Then some rich lady from London comes along and flashes her money in his face and . . ." She lowered her head and dabbed at her eyes.

This was the part Ava hated, but she knew she needed to forge ahead.

"How did your daughter die?"

The woman reached in a drawer and with a delicate hand pulled out a handkerchief.

"My Arianna killed herself," she said, wiping her eyes. "She took her own life. After everything that man did to her, she couldn't bear to go on."

"What did he do?" Ava asked, noting the fact that the woman refused to say Fredericko's name.

"Bled her dry. My father owned a tailor

shop, a very lucrative business. He left the shop to Arianna when he died. Then this snake comes along and whispers these lies in her ears. Not only does he bleed her dry of every nickel she's saved and earned for her own college education, but he has her sign over the deed to her grandfather's shop, then sold it right from underneath all of us. Arianna was devastated. It was my father's legacy. That fiend didn't even apologize. He laughed in her face and told her to get over it. After he's made her broke and penniless, he tells her he's leaving her for another woman."

Ava was dumbfounded by how sordid the tale was. She was hoping for something good on Fredericko, but she never expected this.

"To top it off, my daughter was pregnant with the child we thought she could never have. The stress caused her to lose her baby. It was more than my Arianna could bear."

"Wow, so obviously there's no love lost between you and Fredericko?" Cliff asked.

Ava shot him a look as if to say, *Leave the interviewing to me.*

The woman looked at Cliff like that was the dumbest question she'd ever heard.

"Of course there's no love lost. He's the devil, and I curse the ground he walks on."

85

She paused, recovering from her outburst. "This girl he's marrying, is she your friend?" she asked Ava.

"No, but I interviewed her," Ava replied.

"If I were you, I'd tell her, if she knows what's good for her, she will run as far away from that devil as she can." The woman hesitated again. "But something is fishy." She leaned in and whispered like someone was actually in the shop, listening. "I hear about this marriage. I looked her up. She's a celebrity and worth a lot of money." She slapped her thigh. "I guarantee you that is the only reason he's marrying her. When he bleeds her dry, he will throw her out like yesterday's trash."

Ava's mind started churning as she thought of the way Eli would react to this bombshell. He was going to love this.

"I told my Arianna that he was trash," she went on quietly. "He comes from the slums, and just because some fancy family makes him a charity case and puts him in an exclusive boarding school, it doesn't change that fact. He's still trash."

Ava was having a hard time processing all of this information. She'd hoped for something to work with, and Mrs. Juliette Carlone was giving her almost too much.

"So, he grew up in the slums? Here in

Aruba?"

She nodded. "A poor part of the island called San Nicolas. He was an orphan who was taken in by a very sweet family. His foster mother still lives there. I think, 1113 Damascus Street."

Ava and Cliff exchanged a look. They were both thinking the same thing. They had definitely struck gold.

"Do you mind if I take your picture to go with our story?" Cliff asked, reaching for his bag.

"No, no photos of me," she said, showing a touch of an old woman's vanity. "And not because I care about that man. You print my name." She pointed toward Ava's note-pad. "And you write that I said he's a disgusting excuse of a man and anyone that marries him is a fool. If he wants to send someone to break my legs because of what I say, then so be it." Her shoulders slowly deflated. "My life is not worth living anyway without my Arianna, my lovely child." A tear trickled down her cheek, and Ava knew it was time to wrap up the interview. What was news for the masses was also one woman's heartbreak.

"Well, Mrs. Carlone, my sincerest condolences on your daughter, and I thank you for taking the time to talk with me."

Mrs. Carlone nodded, her anger replaced with a look of deep sadness.

Ava followed Cliff out of the sewing shop. In the half hour they'd been inside, the pedestrian traffic had picked up considerably.

"So, I guess we're catching a cab to San Nicolas?" Cliff said.

"You guessed right," Ava replied, pulling out her cell phone. "But first I need to call Eli. He'll be happy to know I got his blockbuster story."

11

Ultra-handsome Fredericko couldn't have possibly come from this. Ava took in the dilapidated neighborhood. The shanties, which were literally stacked one on top of the other, looked like they would fall over with one good windstorm. Clothes were hanging from some of the balconies, and trash was strewn throughout the streets. Several scrappy-looking men sat around in wooden chairs, bottles of beer at their feet. This was definitely not the Aruba they showed in the travel brochures.

"Is this it?" the driver asked as he slowed in front of a bleached wooden shanty.

Ava glanced down at the piece of paper on which she'd written the address to make sure. "It is," she said to the cabdriver, who was eyeing her skeptically in the rearview mirror. Cliff was wearing that same skepticism.

"I'm not sure nice Americans like you

should be in a place like this," the driver said with a heavy Spanish accent. "It very dangerous."

Ava disagreed. She had a story to track down. It was broad daylight. What could really happen?

"Come on, Cliff," she said, opening the cab door.

"Um, can we have you wait?" Cliff asked, leaning forward. "Just to be on the safe side."

The cabbie turned around in the front seat. "You have American dollars? I do whatever you like."

Cliff folded out three twenties. "We won't be long. There are two more of these if you'll wait."

The unshaven man grinned widely as he grabbed the money. "I'll be right here."

Ava pulled herself out of the backseat of the cab. Cliff was right behind her. "I don't know about this." He eyed two men standing on the porch next door, looking like they were ready to start trouble. "This place doesn't look safe," he whispered.

"You are more than welcome to wait in the cab."

He turned up his nose at the thought. "You know I'm not going to let you do this by yourself."

She smiled, laying a hand on his forearm. "Awww, I have my own personal body-guard."

He returned her smile. "Whatever. I like my job, or at least my paycheck, and I don't want to have to explain to Eli how I watched his new reporter get killed in Aruba."

"Stop being so negative. You can take any of these guys," she said, winking at him before turning and walking up the cracked sidewalk to the shanty. Before she even climbed the porch steps, the door swung open.

"*Sí?*" An elderly woman with long, stringy gray hair peered out at them. Her eyes were sunken and her olive skin was quilted with wrinkles. She was barefoot and wore a long, tattered yellow and blue housecoat.

"Umm, my name is Ava Cole. I'm a U.S. journalist and we're doing a story on Fredericko de la Cruz." She didn't bother introducing Cliff, who was standing behind her like he really was trying to protect her.

The way the woman was staring at her, Ava wasn't sure if she spoke English.

"*Inglés, sí?*" Ava asked. She knew a lot of Arubans spoke Papiamento, a form of Spanish. She hoped they didn't speak Dutch, Aruba's official language, because she didn't know a lick of Dutch.

The old woman continued to stare, a scowl plastered on her face. Ava wondered if she still had all her marbles.

Suddenly a young, pretty woman appeared behind her. She was in her early twenties, with long, black hair and piercing gray eyes. "Go back inside, *madushi*. I'll handle her."

The woman turned up her nose, then began muttering something in her native tongue. By the way her hands flailed, Ava figured she probably wasn't saying anything pleasant.

The young woman stepped into the doorway. "My grandmother does not speak English too well. What can we help you with?"

Ava shifted nervously. "I'm just looking for people who might have known Fredericko de la Cruz when he lived here."

Ava thought she saw a flash of panic pass over the woman's face.

"Please, I won't take but a few minutes of your time," Ava quickly said. The woman looked like she was going to slam the door closed at any moment. "I was told you might be able to help me find out a little more about him, or perhaps put me in touch with someone who could."

The young woman looked around nervously, then said, "Fredericko has no family. He was an orphan."

"I know that, but I was wondering if I could talk to his foster mother."

Ava heard the old woman suddenly begin screaming from inside the house. She couldn't make out what the woman was saying, but she did hear her say "Fredericko" and *"djablo,"* which Ava assumed was the Papiamento term for *devil.*

The young woman turned around and yelled to her grandmother, *"Madushi, para!"* Whatever she said settled the old woman down, because the screaming stopped. She turned back to face Ava. "Look, we can't help you."

She began to retreat, and Ava stuck her foot in the door. "Please, just a couple more questions. I know he lived here as a child, but then he left to go to boarding school?"

The woman sighed. She must have decided that the sooner she gave Ava the information she needed, the sooner Ava would leave because she said, "He lived here. But he was sent away when he was thirteen. He was too much for my family to handle. He had some fancy Dutch family come along and enroll him in a boarding school in London."

So that explained Fredericko's taste for

the finer things in life. "Did he ever come back here from London?"

The woman didn't hide her irritation. "Yes, he moved back after boarding school, but he was still trouble. He stole from my family every chance he could get."

"I'm sorry," Ava said, processing all that the young woman was saying. "That seems so out of character for him. He seems so, I don't know, refined."

For the first time, the woman allowed a smile. "Fredericko always was a good actor."

Ava made a note to herself: that line was a keeper. "Do you know he's about to get married?"

"Everyone knows. He, as you Americans say, has hit pay dirt. Again."

Another great line, Ava thought. "Is that what everyone here believes? And what do you mean, again?"

"You ask a lot of questions," the woman said.

Ava shrugged. "I'm a journalist. It's my job."

The old woman began loudly fussing again and the smile left the young woman's face. "Look, I've already said too much. Fredericko, he's not nice when you cross him. We leave him alone and he leaves us alone. If you know what's good for you, you will leave him alone, too. Fredericko doesn't like when anyone meddles in his affairs."

Ava wasn't stopping now. "I'll take my chances."

"No, I've said enough, now go." The woman slammed the door and locked it before Ava could say another word.

Ava stood stock-still on the porch, wondering if she should knock again.

"Look, you've got terrific dirt, now let's go!" Cliff said. Ava was about to protest until she looked on the other side of the shanty where several nosy old men were glaring her way. The scary-looking guys had already come down off their porch, like wolves closing in on their prey.

Cliff didn't give her time to reply as he grabbed her and pulled her toward the waiting cab. She had to admit, she felt a sense of relief once they piled inside and the cabdriver sped away.

"I see why you won all those awards," Cliff said, once they were cruising back toward the hotel. "You're relentless, you know that?"

She leaned back against the seat. "How do you know I've won awards?"

He tapped his head. "I may be just a photographer, but I know how to do a little investigating of my own. I needed to know who I would be hanging out with in Aruba."

The more she found out about Cliff, the more she liked him. "Well, yeah, some people have said I'm a little relentless. I just try to get the story." She pulled out her notepad and began writing. "And this is definitely a story."

They had left behind the shanties and pulled into the island's lone highway. "Fredericko seems to strike terror in people," she said, making a list. "Which means he's probably ruthless."

"Let's not forget he was poor, orphaned, and a thief."

She nodded. "And today he still doesn't have a job." She stopped writing. "So why in the world would India marry someone like that?"

"That's the million-dollar question," Cliff said. "India is worth millions, so she had to have done her homework. From what I can tell, he has nothing to offer. So, why would a superstar like India give him the time of day?"

Ava leaned back in her seat. That was the question she needed answered. Her gut told her that if she could find out the answer to that question, she'd get the blockbuster story of the year. Suddenly, an idea popped into her head. She leaned forward.

"Hey, can you take us by the nearest police station?" she asked the driver.

"I take you wherever you need to go." He rubbed his fingers together. "Especially if you have more money."

Ava reached in her pocket, pulled out another twenty, and handed it to him.

"Why are we going to the police station?" Cliff asked.

Ava pointed down at her notepad. "With Fredericko's history, I'd be willing to bet he has a police record. I'm sure that can lead us somewhere."

Cliff nodded, impressed. "Girl, you're better than good."

She shrugged off his comment. "Let's just hope we can turn up something."

Ava's adrenaline was racing now. She was onto a lead, and she wouldn't be able to stop until she found out where it went. In the space of a morning she had uncovered all sorts of pieces to the puzzle. This Fredericko was a conniving lowlife. Her visit to the local gendarmes might turn up even worse. Yet she still needed the key: What did India see in this rat?

12

The police station was located in Santa Cruz. Ava didn't know what she would find, but she wanted to at least try. She'd been lucky so far. Maybe she could find a rap sheet a mile long.

"Here you go," the cabdriver said, pulling up in front of a large, yellow building that looked like a hotel. "You want me to wait?"

"Please," Cliff said, peeling off another twenty.

The cabdriver grinned widely as he took the money. "Of course, my friend. I wait right here."

Ava and Cliff climbed out of the car and went inside. She headed to the front desk, where a middle-aged blond woman was tapping on a computer. A uniformed officer stood over her, pointing to something on the screen.

"Excuse me," Ava said, flashing a smile. Both the man and woman looked up at her.

"My name is Ava Cole. I'm an American journalist, and I'm wondering if I can get some information on a Fredericko de la Cruz, perhaps see if he has a criminal record."

The woman looked to the man, whose stoic face hardened.

"Ummm, *se hable inglés?*" Ava said.

"I speak English just fine," the officer said. "I'm just wondering why you think I'd give that information to you."

"Because isn't it public record?"

He continued to stare at her without responding.

Ava was not intimidated by the police. "I can file an open records request if I need to, but I was thinking it would be easier if I could take a look at it here."

"We don't have public records. That information is need-to-know. And you don't need to know." The officer spun and walked away.

Ava's mouth dropped open. "How rude," she said, turning back to Cliff.

He shrugged. "Well, it was a good idea."

Ava sighed, not wanting to admit defeat. She didn't know Aruba law, so she didn't know if the issue was even worth fighting. "Forget it. Let's go," she said, deciding that she had enough to work with.

They had just reached the taxi when the blond officer who had been sitting behind the front desk caught up with them. "Hey," she said in a hushed whisper.

"Yes?" Ava said, stopping and turning toward her.

She looked around nervously. "I could give you information on Fredericko."

Ava's eyes lit up. "You could?"

The woman nodded. "You have money?"

Ava checked Cliff's reaction. Normally in this situation she'd tell the subject to take a hike, but she was with the *Star* now. The rules were different. Cliff looked mildly bored.

"Yes, I do. How's a thousand dollars?" Ava shook off the disgusting feeling that arose from offering money in exchange for a story.

The woman shifted, her eyes opening wide. "American dollars?"

Ava nodded.

"Make it two thousand."

Ava looked to Cliff again. He subtly nodded to let her know that amount would be fine.

"Two thousand it is."

"In twenty minutes, meet me at the Fondango shopping strip, three blocks from here. Your driver will know where it is." She motioned toward the cab. "Twenty minutes.

Bring the cash." She turned and ran back inside.

Ava turned back to Cliff.

"Is that really okay?"

Cliff started to laugh. "Two thousand is chicken feed. I was expecting her to start at ten thousand."

Ava felt a little naïve herself. "Well, we still have a problem. Where are we supposed to get two thousand dollars in twenty minutes?"

"Well, you have fifteen hundred back in the room, don't you?"

She'd forgotten about that money. "Oh yeah."

"So we go pick that up. We don't have time to have Eli wire anything, so I'll just get a cash advance on my card for the other five."

They jumped back in the taxi and had him take them to the hotel. Exactly twenty minutes later, they were waiting in the shopping strip.

The blond policewoman pulled up next to them in a small foreign car. She rolled down her window. "Get in," she ordered.

Ava didn't say anything as she climbed out of the cab. Cliff immediately began getting out of the other side.

"No, just you," she told Ava.

Ava held up her hand to let Cliff know she would be fine. He looked uneasy, but after all, it was a policewoman.

Once Ava got in, the woman let out a long sigh and heaved back in her seat. She removed her shades and head scarf. "Look, let's make this quick. Aruba is a small place and if anyone finds out I gave you this information, I'm in big trouble. I could lose my job. Not to mention what Fredericko would do."

"Nobody will find out," Ava said firmly. The *National Star* prided itself on the fact that no one *ever* revealed their sources. Eli had made that clear from the beginning. That's why the company was always able to get good stories, because people knew their identities would remain a secret.

"All right." The woman huffed. "You got my money?"

Ava felt like a drug buyer as she reached in the small purse she had strapped around her waist and pulled out the money.

The woman snatched the envelope and tore it open. Her eyes lit up at the sight of the wad of cash. She quickly counted it. "Let's get this over with," she said after she was done and had tucked the money in her bag.

Ava held up her recorder. "Do you mind

if I record this? I don't have to identify you."

"If you must," the woman snapped.

Ava pulled out her notepad as well. She had learned in journalism school to always take notes and not rely on a tape recorder, even in this digital age. She pressed Record and readied herself to write. "Okay, tell me what you know. How do you know Fredericko?"

"That's irrelevant," the woman said. "Just trust. I do know him very well, and there is nothing legitimate about him. That's why even though I'm not supposed to have access to his files, I knew he had an extensive rap sheet." She reached into a straw bag in the backseat, pulled out a thick stack of papers, and handed it to Ava. "This is his arrest record." She pointed to the paper on top. "It dates back to when he was thirteen and arrested for assault of his foster mother. He's been in trouble for everything from grand larceny to fraud to impersonating a soldier."

"Wow," Ava said, perusing the papers. "This guy is a piece of work."

"And then some," the woman said. "You should find everything you need to know about his criminal background in those papers. Now I have to go."

"Can I get your name?"

"No. I have to go." She put her glasses back on.

Ava tucked the papers under her arm, then opened the car door and stepped out. "Thank you, you've definitely given me something to work with."

"Just remember, you never talked to me." The woman started her car.

"Who are you again?" Ava said, pushing for a name.

The woman floored the accelerator and roared off. Ava strolled back over to the cab.

"So?" Cliff said.

"I'll tell you at the hotel," she said, eyeing the driver.

Cliff didn't protest the wait. From the smile on Ava's face, he knew Ava had turned up what they were looking for.

13

Cliff and Ava had barely entered the hotel lobby when they heard Mia call out, "Yoo-hoo!"

They looked over at the bar, where Mia was perched, a piña colada in her hand.

Ava cut her eyes at Cliff. "My little sister beckons."

Cliff laughed. "Go deal with your sister. I'm exhausted from all the sun. I'm going upstairs to take a nap."

They said their good-byes and Ava made her way over to the bar.

"What are you doing?" she asked Mia.

As Mia swung around on the bar stool, the slit in her sundress revealed a long, sultry leg. "What does it look like?" She held up her glass. "Having a drink." She motioned toward the sexy bartender. "And enjoying the atmosphere." Mia took a sip of her drink, closed her eyes, and purred as the liquor went down. "That is soooo good.

Where have you been all day? I'm ready to have some fun."

"I *am* working," Ava said. "Hence the reason I didn't invite you to come down with me."

"Ohh, poo." She playfully stuck out her bottom lip. "I need to find someone to play with here. You're no fun."

"Let me repeat, I'm working."

"Speaking of working," she said, grinning excitedly, "when are you going to introduce me to India?"

"I'm not." Ava sat down in the seat next to her sister and motioned to the bartender. "May I have a piña colada also?"

The bartender flashed a sexy smile. "Coming right up."

"I didn't fly all the way here not to meet India," Mia continued, pulling on her sister's arm. "My sister has an inside connection, and you think I'm not going to meet her? Please, this is my destiny."

Ava wasn't going to be badgered on this point. "I'm a professional. What would I look like walking up to India and saying, 'Hey, this is my little sister. Can you give her a job?' "

"You'd look like . . . Oh, never mind," she said as she spotted something over Ava's shoulder. "I'll introduce myself to her."

Before Ava could say another word, Mia was bouncing over to a small group of people who had just gotten off the elevator. Julian and the nerdy-looking man Ava had seen them come in with stepped out, followed by India and Fredericko.

"Mia!" Ava hissed as she followed her sister.

Mia ignored her as she approached the pop star. "India!" she called out. The burly bodyguard immediately put a hand up to stop Mia from getting too close.

"Excuse me," Mia said, eyeing his hand, which was placed palm out on her chest.

He immediately dropped his hand. "Sorry, ma'am, but Miss Wright doesn't want to be disturbed."

Mia waggled her head, showing she was not like that. "Sir, I am not some googly-eyed fan. I am a highly trained professional, and I need to talk to Miss Wright about how my services can benefit her."

India smiled briefly, then waved as she and Fredericko ducked out the side door. The bodyguard flashed a "take that" smirk, then followed them out.

"Well, ain't that some mess?" Mia said, her hands going to her hips.

"Would you please not embarrass me?" Ava said, coming up.

Before Mia could respond, Julian and the other man approached them.

"Hi, Ava," Julian said warmly.

"Hi, Julian," Ava replied.

Mia still had a scowl on her face as she pointed at Julian. "Are you with —"

"Mia," Ava said, quickly interrupting, "this is Julian, India's manager, and, I'm sorry, I didn't catch your name," she told the other man.

He smiled sheepishly as he extended his hand to Mia. "I'm Felix Spaulding, India's accountant. Nice to meet you, ma'am."

Any anger Mia had felt over missing her chance to meet India dissipated as she smiled playfully. "Ma'am? Do I look like a ma'am?"

"No, no. I didn't mean to offend you," he said, a worried look crossing his face. "I just —"

Mia gently touched his arm. "I was just kidding."

"Oh, sorry," he said, pushing his glasses up on his nose.

"Look here," Julian said, "I would like to steal your sister now. My schedule freed up earlier than I thought, so why don't we begin our date now?"

Mia cocked her head, eyeing Ava severely. "Umm, sissy. Look at you. You didn't tell me you had a date."

"Well, she does. So do you mind if I steal her away?"

Ava definitely wanted to spend time with Julian, but after being gone all day, she didn't want her sister complaining. "Well, Mia and I were going to —"

Felix interrupted. "I'd be happy to keep Mia entertained."

Ava wanted to laugh because Felix was so not her sister's type. He was tall but very lanky. He had curly black hair and was about as average-looking as they came. And although he'd shed his suit, he still wore a button-up short-sleeve shirt, khakis, and penny loafers. Her sister would never go for someone who wore penny loafers. Ava was just about to open her mouth and say something so her sister wouldn't be put on the spot when she saw a bright smile light up Mia's face.

"I'd like that," Mia said.

"What? Are you sure?" Ava asked.

Mia draped her arm through Felix's. "I am. I need to get my financial house in order. Maybe Mr. Spaulding can share some tips on how I can make that happen."

"Of course," he said eagerly.

"See, your sister is all taken care of," Julian said.

"I guess so." Ava looked down at her outfit. She was hot and sweaty from being out all day. "Okay, then. But can I have about fifteen minutes to change?"

"You sure can. I'll go ahead and get us a table in the restaurant."

Ava looked over at her sister one last time. "Are you sure you'll be okay?"

Mia waved off her sister as she turned to Felix. "Someone forgot to tell my sister she didn't give birth to me." With her lacquered fingernails she pulled Felix away. "Bye, sissy, see you when I see you."

"She'll be fine," Julian said. "And I'll be right here."

Ava smiled, then darted upstairs to change. After five long years on the shelf, she was going to be wined and dined. "I think," she said softly as she entered the empty elevator, "I could get used to this."

14

Ava tried to put the dizzying thoughts of her sister out of her head as Julian stood to greet her.

"Hi there," he said, leaning in to kiss her on the cheek. "You look stunning." He looked at his watch. "And it only took you forty-five minutes."

Her mouth dropped open. "Was I gone that long?"

"No, I'm kidding," he said, pulling her chair out for her. "It was only about twenty minutes."

Ava didn't miss his eyes roaming her body. She silently patted herself on the back for thinking to drop this sexy espresso wrap dress in her suitcase at the last minute. It hugged her in all the right places and was one of the most flattering pieces she owned. She'd pinned up her shoulder-length light brown hair, leaving just enough curls to frame her face. She was sure the bronze shimmering powder she'd dusted on her cheeks radiated against her skin.

"You look nice as well," she said. And he did in his linen button-down shirt, khakis, and Italian loafers.

"I took the liberty of ordering us some Dom Pérignon."

Ava felt her heart flutter. He had expensive tastes on top of being handsome.

"I know you're worried about your sister," Julian said as Ava took her seat. "But, if it makes you feel any better, Felix really is a stand-up guy. A little too rigid for my taste, a by-the-book fella. But hey, when you have someone handling millions of your dollars, I guess that's the kind of person you want."

That was refreshing to hear. At least Ava didn't have to worry about her sister going off on the island with some deranged rock star groupie.

"You know what?" Ava said. "How about we talk about something else? My little sister only gets my nerves worked up."

"She does seem like a little fireball." Julian picked up his glass of champagne and leaned back. "Well, tell me about yourself."

Ava took a sip of champagne, then proceeded to do just that. They ordered dinner, then talked for the next two hours about everything under the sun. She was surprised to learn that someone like him was single, but he said working for India didn't allow for much time to get to know women.

After dinner, they chatted some more before the conversation turned to her story.

"How did the interview with India go?" Julian asked.

She hesitated, not sure if she should be truthful. "Well, it wasn't exactly what I was hoping for. It was, how do I say it, careful?"

He laughed. "That's my India. Everything is carefully crafted."

"Yeah, I know, but . . ." Ava weighed her words carefully. "Can I ask you something? And you don't have to answer if you don't want to. But why do you think she would marry Fredericko without a prenup?" She hesitated, and for a moment Ava wished she could take her words back. The last thing she wanted to do was turn him off or make him think that she had gone out with him to dig up info on India.

Julian didn't seem fazed by her question. "I've asked myself that question many times. Yet despite what people may think, Fredericko is a cool guy and he does love India. As her manager, I've tried to advise her not to let love make her foolish. It's part of the reason I had Felix come on the trip; I was hoping he could get through to her before she actually said 'I do.' "

"So you're comfortable with her marrying Fredericko?"

He nodded pensively. "I am. I think he'll make her very happy. I don't think she should be a fool and marry him without a prenup. Contrary to people's belief, he does have a little money of his own." Julian held up his hands. "Don't ask me how he got it, but he does have his own bankroll. The bottom line for me is, I don't have to live with him. If she's happy, so am I."

Ava realized he didn't know of Fredericko's criminal history. "Well, maybe you or Felix can get through to India. I really don't want to get all up in her personal business, but I've seen enough divorces to know that a person worth millions would definitely want to protect herself. And I did a little digging today and found out some facts about her intended that hammer home the need for that prenup."

"Yeah, what type of things?" he asked, alarmed, and Ava immediately wondered if she'd said too much. She set down her champagne. The wine was making her too loose-lipped.

Ava contemplated whether she should share what she'd dug up so far. Since she planned to let India know what she'd found, she decided to go ahead and share.

"Well, I found out that Fredericko is a real piece of work. He has a criminal background dating back to his youth and he has made a habit of stalking wealthy women."

Julian leaned back, shocked by the news. "Wow. I definitely didn't know that."

Ava nodded. "Yeah, and did you know he's been married twice?"

"I knew about one wife, but two?" Julian shook his head. "And you've learned all this in your short time on the island?"

She opened her hands slightly. "I guess you can say I'm pretty good at what I do."

"I guess so, huh?"

They chatted some more before Ava realized that it was after ten o'clock. She hadn't written one word of her bombshell article yet.

"You know, this has been great, but I'd better get upstairs and get some work done."

Julian sat up straight. "Yeah, you and me both." He paid the check and they continued to talk as they made their way to the elevator. He'd agreed that she should let India know what she'd found out as soon as possible, and he even offered to help arrange another meeting.

When the elevator opened on Ava's floor,

she was surprised that he got off with her. He must've noticed her tense up because he said, "I just wanted to walk you to your room." He hesitated just the right amount. "Unless, of course, you want me to come in."

She did want him to come in, but she wasn't sure she was ready. She found herself saying, "We'd better call it a night here."

A defeated look crossed his face. "Are you sure? Because I'm not quite ready to call it a night." He leaned in, and before she knew it, he had planted a deep and sensuous kiss on her lips. It sent sparks shooting through her body and she felt herself getting moist.

Ava gently pulled back. "I'm sure." She swallowed hard and said more forcefully, like she was trying to convince herself, "Yes, I'm sure, I'm sure."

He smiled casually. "Maybe next time, then. Sweet dreams, Miss Ava Cole."

He waved sexily as he headed back toward the elevator. Ava knew that if she spent much more time with Julian, she wouldn't be able to continue telling him no.

15

Around 6 A.M., loud voices in the hallway woke Ava. Normally, she wouldn't have paid any attention, but she immediately recognized the high-pitched giggle. What in the world was Mia doing up and out this early?

Ava stuck her head out her hotel door and was shocked to see a tipsy Mia being led down the hallway by Felix.

She pushed the lock open to keep her door from closing and stepped out into the hall. "Mia! Are you just getting in?" Ava exclaimed.

"Heeeey, sissy," Mia said. "Aruba is so much fun!" She wasn't slurring her words, which meant she wasn't drunk, but she was definitely buzzing.

Ava turned her attention to Felix, who looked apologetic. "Sorry for keeping your sister out all night."

"What are you apologizing to her for?" Mia asked. "She's not my mother." She playfully slapped Felix's shoulder. "Although sometimes I don't think she knows that."

"Do you have any idea what time it is?" Ava asked.

Mia shrugged. "I'm on vacation. I have no need to be concerned about the time."

Felix stepped up like he felt the need to explain. "We, um, we wanted to watch the sunrise on the beach."

Mia leaned over and draped her hands through his. "It was Felix's suggestion. It was so romantic. You know, I've never seen a sunrise."

That brought a smile to Felix's face.

"Well, come on, I need you to tuck me in," Mia said, stepping around her sister.

Ava stepped in front of her to block her path. "I can help you get to bed," she said sternly.

Mia rolled her eyes. "I wish you would stop —"

"It's okay," Felix interrupted. "I'm going to go catch a few hours of sleep myself. I have a meeting this morning."

"You don't have to run off because of my sister," Mia said.

Felix smiled reassuringly. "No, it's okay. She probably wants to make sure you're fine. So we'll catch up later today?"

She touched a sexy finger to his chest. "I'm looking forward to it."

Felix continued smiling as he backed away. No sooner had the elevator doors closed behind him than Mia spun on her sister. "Do you always have to be a cock blocker?"

"You do not need to be sleeping with that man, who, need I remind you, you just met."

"First of all, don't tell me who I need to be sleeping with. I'm grown. Didn't you get the memo? Second of all, that's your problem — you always have to adhere to a certain standard. You have to date a guy three-point-two months before you'll sleep with him. Third, you can't date coworkers. Relax and just live some, why don't you?" Mia stumbled around her sister and headed to her room. "I'm going to bed."

"Mia!" Ava said, following her sister. "I'm not trying to run your life. But Fredericko is a criminal, and you need to watch yourself around anyone associated with him."

"Felix has nothing to do with Fredericko. He works for India." Mia waved her off and pulled out her room key. "Besides, that argument is moot, seeing as how you're all up in Julian's face."

Ava sighed in frustration. She didn't follow her sister inside her room. She couldn't deal with Mia right now. Her sister could be incorrigible, especially after she had a drink in her system.

Ava returned to her room and crawled back into bed. Enough about Mia, she told herself. Ava had a job to do. She sure hoped she'd get a chance to talk to India today. If not, she needed to see what else, if anything, she could dig up. Her mind raced until she dozed off. She awoke about an hour later when her cell phone rang.

"Hello," she said, not bothering to look at the caller ID.

"Ava Cole?"

"Yes?"

"Hi, this is Chuck Maddison from NBC News."

Ava bolted upright in bed. She'd been trying to get on with NBC's investigative show *Dateline* for the past two years. But those positions rarely opened, and since she didn't have a television background, she'd all but given up hope.

"Yes, sir, Mr. Maddison."

"Did I catch you at a bad time? You sound like you may be sleeping."

"Oh, no, no. I'm fine," she said, tossing back the covers and sitting on the edge of the bed. "I'm actually on assignment in Aruba."

"Oh, I'm sorry. I'll make this quick since you're on international rates."

"No problem. What can I do for you?"

"Well, I saw Sebastian, your old boss, recently, and he told me you'd moved over to the *National Star.*"

She wanted to say, "unfortunately," but instead said, "Yes. I'm actually here for the *Star* now, doing a story on India Wright."

"The pop star?"

"The one and only."

"Well, I'm sure whatever you're digging up is scandalous."

If only you knew, Ava thought.

"Well, I know you just started there, but I was wondering if you were still interested in the network job."

She wanted to scream, "What do you think?"

"Of course," she offered eagerly. "My contract has a noncompete out, so I would just have to give them thirty days' notice."

"Whoa, there's nothing official yet. We just had someone take early retirement, and Sebastian thought you'd be a fit for the job."

"I would," she said quickly.

"Great. Will you be back in town next week? I'd love to have you come in and talk with a few people."

"Definitely. Just let me know when."

"All right, my secretary will be back in touch." His voice turned thoughtful as he added, "I know someone of your caliber is probably having a hard time adjusting to that tabloid world." Finally, someone who understood her pain. "But just put those investigative skills to work and bring home a great story. We'll be watching the magazine to see what you come up with."

They exchanged good-byes and Ava leaned back, still unable to believe that the network had finally called. Still, that meant the pressure was on. Even though she was in the tabloid arena, good investigative skills were good investigative skills, no matter what. So now, more than ever, she had to bring home a blockbuster story.

16

As Ava nibbled on the last of her toast, she eyed her watch one more time. She was waiting on twelve o'clock. Julian had held true to his word, and right after the call from the network, India's assistant, Jackie, called, agreeing to give Ava five minutes at noon, right before India's spa treatment.

Ava was still giddy about the job offer, but right now she had to focus on the best way to approach this story. She'd had two sources confirming that Fredericko was no good, but the real story would be whether India knew, and if so, why would she marry someone like that?

At ten minutes till twelve, Ava rose and made her way back to the elevators. She pressed the Up button, then stood back and waited for the doors to open. When they did, her mouth dropped open. Fredericko stepped off, almost walking into her. He lost his smile when he recognized who she was.

"Excuse me," he said, making an exaggerated turn around her.

"Ummm, hey, can I talk to you for a moment?" Ava said, turning to follow him.

"I'm sorry, but I leave all the press to my fiancée," he said, speeding up to escape.

Ava fast-walked to catch up with him. "I understand that, but I was just hoping that maybe you could answer a couple of questions for me."

"I'm very busy."

Yeah, late for golf, she thought, eyeing his crisp golf khakis and Ralph Lauren polo shirt.

"Yes, again, I understand that," Ava said, matching his steps. "But I was wondering if you could tell me about your ex-wife. I mean, wives."

That caused him to stop in his tracks. He spun toward her. "I have no idea what you're talking about," he hissed. Yet the anger creases in his forehead told her that she had touched a nerve.

"So you don't know Arianna, or Lady Von Haven of London?" She'd done her homework last night to find the name of the London woman he'd married.

He looked like he wanted to strangle her right there in the hotel lobby.

"Aren't you supposed to be here covering

India?" he asked nastily.

"I'm more interested in India's soon-to-be husband," she replied.

"Look, lady," Fredericko said, losing his smooth demeanor and sexy Latin accent, "I don't know what kind of garbage-gathering reporter you call yourself." He took a step toward her, until he was so close she could feel the heat of his breath. "But if I were you, I'd be very, very careful before going around listening to town gossip. Now, I told you, I don't know what you're talking about."

Ava didn't back down. "I talked with Arianna's mother." She let that sink in for a moment. "She confirmed the marriage. And I'm sure it won't be that hard to get your marriage to Lady Von Haven confirmed as well."

Fredericko scowled at her again as his nostrils flared.

"Look, I know there are two sides to every story. All I'm asking for is your side," Ava continued. "Or I can just talk to India."

As soon as she said that, he grabbed her arm and pinned her against the wall. The move caught Ava off guard, and the rage she saw in his eyes frightened her.

"You nosy little bitch, I will say this again. Mind your business. Get your little feel-good story on the wedding and leave it alone, or I promise you, you will regret it."

As scared as she was, Ava would not let it show. As an investigative reporter, she'd had her share of threats. If Fredericko thought he could bully her into not doing the story, he was like every other loser she'd nailed.

"Get your hands off me before I scream at the top of my lungs," she said calmly.

It must've dawned on him that they were still in the hotel lobby because he slowly released her arm, took a step back, and composed himself.

"Miss Cole," he said with restrained fury, "I would highly recommend you do the job you came here to do. Stay out of the slums. Trust me, Aruba is not a place where a sweet, vulnerable woman like yourself should go wandering off. It's nothing for a pretty young thing such as yourself to come up missing. And I assure you, I am not a man you want to cross."

"Is that a threat?"

"It's a fact." He glared at her one last time, then spun and walked off.

"So, I take it that means you have no comment for my story," she called out after him. She couldn't be sure, but it looked like he was shooting his middle finger at her as he walked away.

17

Ava took a deep breath as her hand gripped the knob. Once she opened this door, there was no turning back.

Her adrenaline was flowing, knowing that she was on to a good story. Seeing Fredericko's reaction proved that. She felt the rush she normally did whenever she pursued an investigative piece. She wasn't intimidated by his threats. If anything, they only fueled her desire to get to the bottom of this story. She had to get answers — answers that could come only from India.

Ava had been pumped on the elevator ride up, but now, as she stood outside India's suite, her stomach felt uneasy. In the past, she'd done stories on greedy corporations stepping on the little people. Her stories had purpose. What purpose was this really serving? She was about to ruin this woman's life, smash her dreams of happily ever after, and expose her fiancé as a con man.

Ava shook off the thoughts. No, she had a job to do. She couldn't get sidetracked by a conscience. Besides, she really was doing India a favor. A man like that would only bring her misery.

Ava inhaled deeply, then knocked. She heard shuffling on the other side of the door. Then a female voice said, "Who is it?"

Ava swallowed. "It's Ava Cole, the reporter, from, uh . . . the reporter from the *National Star.*" Even though she was in her assignment full throttle, she still didn't feel comfortable announcing her place of employment.

The door swung open. India's assistant, Jackie, stood with a scowl on her face.

"You will have five minutes," she said before stomping off.

Ava assumed she was supposed to follow. Jackie pushed open the adjacent double doors to the sitting area. India was staring out of the tall floor-to-ceiling window. This suite was different from the one they'd done the interview in. With its oversize leather furniture, Berber carpet, and contemporary decorations, this was no doubt the presidential penthouse.

"Do you want me to stay?" Jackie asked.

India shook her head, and Jackie eased the doors closed as she backed out, making sure she shot Ava one last disgusted look.

India didn't greet Ava as she turned to walk over to the chaise longue, where she took a seat. She seemed to know that since Ava had returned, she could only be bearing bad news. India picked up her glass of lemonade and took a sip. Finally, she said, "How can I help you?"

Ava wasn't sure if she should take a seat as well, but since India didn't offer, she remained standing. "I don't quite know how to say this," Ava began, "but I have learned some news about Fredericko, and I wanted to see if you would go on record with a response." She paused. "And if not, I at least, woman to woman, wanted to let you know what was going on."

India didn't respond, and Ava pulled out her notepad.

"I'm not sure if you know, but Fredericko has already been married. Twice," Ava began, flipping the pad open. She wanted to make sure she had all her facts together.

India hesitated, not bothering to hide her irritation. "I know that. He told me," she said bluntly.

Ava nodded. She had a feeling that Fredericko had shared some things with his wife-to-be, but he couldn't have possibly told her everything, or why would India be marrying him?

"Well, I don't know if you know, but he's also been accused of forgery, money laundering, and theft. He had two forgery charges for conning women out of their money." Ava waited for a look of disbelief to cross India's face, and she was shocked when India remained emotionless.

"What do you want from me?" India finally said.

"Well, I'm doing a story."

"Fredericko was cleared of all those charges," India said, walking over to the window again.

Ava hesitated, not knowing what she should do next. "So, you're okay with his history?"

India stared out the window, her back to Ava. "There was something about you when you were interviewing me that didn't feel right," India said, seemingly to herself.

"I'm sorry you feel that way. But I'm just doing my job."

India turned and glared, her gaze burning a hole in Ava. "So your job is digging into other people's lives?"

"I'm sorry you had to find out like this. But isn't it better you found out now, before Fredericko wiped you out?"

India slammed her glass down on the end

table so hard, Ava was sure it would shatter. "How do you know what's better for me? You don't know anything about me!"

The violence of the outburst caught Ava by surprise. Yet in India's eyes was a look of pain.

"I know that you're about to marry a con man," Ava gently replied.

India took a deep breath to calm herself down. "Maybe I know all about Fredericko. Maybe I believe in second chances."

That statement caused Ava's eyes to widen in shock. So India was marrying this man knowing all of this about him? Ava reached for her digital recorder in her pocket. "Do you mind giving an official statement?" she said, pulling it out.

She was just about to ask for permission to record when India said, "Put that thing away."

"But I . . ."

"Put it away!" India hissed.

Ava eased the recorder back into her pocket. She debated pushing Record and secretly taping the conversation, but she decided against it. She'd violated a lot of her own work ethics already. She couldn't do that as well.

India began pacing across the room.

"Look, I know who Fredericko is, and *what* he is."

Ava couldn't make sense of this. "Then why in the world would you marry him?"

"Because," India replied, swallowing hard, "I don't have a choice."

"What do you mean, you don't have a choice?"

She stopped and studied Ava again. Her expression was that of a woman who bore many secrets, yet who was also tired and ready to come clean.

"I know people think I'm some dumb pop star, but I'm savvy enough to know what I'm dealing with," India said. "I know everything there is to know about the man I'm about to marry."

Ava couldn't believe what she was hearing. "How, then, could you possibly still want to marry him? Do you love him that much?"

India started to snort, but then caught herself. "Look, it's none of your business how much I love my soon-to-be husband. I'm marrying him and that's all there is to it."

Ava was dumbfounded. This wasn't adding up. "Look, I don't like having to do this, but I will. My gut is telling me you're leaving something out. Either you shoot straight with me, or I won't have any choice but to do a complete exposé."

India's bravado momentarily disappeared, and if Ava knew how to read people at all, she would say India was distressed. But India quickly pulled herself together, stomped over to the door, and flung it open.

"You do what you have to do. If you get joy out of destroying people's lives, then so be it."

Ava didn't say anything as she walked over to the door. Her eyes shifted down to India's hand, which was gripping the doorknob. Her hand was shaking. Their eyes met. Ava expected to see scorn. Instead, all she saw was fear.

As she stepped out into the hallway, she was more sure than ever that something else was going on. She just had to dig a little deeper and find out what that was.

Fredericko, who seemed to loom larger-than-life on the island, had some hold on his future bride.

18

Ava was surprised that Julian still wanted to go out for a walk on the beach. After everything that had transpired with India, she expected Julian to bail on their rendez-vous. So when he'd shown up at her hotel room door an hour earlier, she hadn't even been dressed. He'd waited for her to get changed so they could enjoy a romantic walk.

"Thank you for letting me be the one to tell India about Fredericko and for persuading her to agree to talk to me again," Ava said.

"Not a problem. What was her reaction?"

"I guess you're right. I guess she loves him enough to overlook all the negatives about him. But . . ." She stopped herself. Although she liked Julian, he was still India's manager. She decided not to lay all of her cards on the table and tell him her hunch that India was hiding something. Instead she said,

"But this evening is about relaxing. Just hanging out with you."

"I'm looking forward to a relaxing evening with you," Julian told her as they walked hand in hand through the hotel lobby. "I really enjoyed talking to you last night."

"I enjoyed talking to you, too," Ava replied. She probably shouldn't be getting involved with someone so soon after Phillip, but it felt like they'd broken up months ago. "I know you're busy, so I wasn't sure if this —"

"Julian!"

Both Ava and Julian turned to face the voice yelling their way. Jackie rushed up behind them with a scowl on her face. Ava realized that this woman didn't like reporters, but she took her disdain to a whole different level.

"Yes, Jackie?" Julian said. "What is it?"

"Felix needs you," she said, not bothering to acknowledge Ava.

"Well, Felix is going to have to wait," Julian informed her. "I'm off duty for a minute."

"Where are you going?" Jackie asked.

"We're in Aruba. I'm going out to enjoy myself," he responded.

She scanned Ava from head to toe. "We are here for work, you know?"

"Can I get some relaxation time?" Julian asked.

"Not today," she said with a smirk. "You are India's manager, and you need to come manage some things. I've been sent to find you. So your little friend is going to have to take a rain check."

He let out an exasperated sigh. "What is it now?"

"Felix has some questions about India's finances. You really need to come see him so you can answer them," Jackie said flatly.

"Can't this wait?"

"Obviously not, if they sent me to find you."

Julian blew out a frustrated breath, then looked at Ava apologetically. "I'm sorry, but it looks like I'm going to have to cancel on you."

Ava tried not to let her disappointment show. "No, I understand. Duty calls."

"Yeah, duty calls," Jackie repeated with an edge.

"Hey, how about I take you to breakfast tomorrow morning around nine?" Julian said.

"Yeah, that sounds good." She half expected him to lean in and kiss her goodbye, but instead he gave her hand a friendly squeeze, then headed toward the elevator.

Jackie scowled at her again, then followed behind him.

"Well, great," Ava mumbled, looking around the hotel lobby. "All dressed up and no place to play." She had a beautiful evening ahead of her and nothing to do.

Ava decided to take Cliff up on his offer to hang out, so she walked over to the hotel's house phone and called his room. When he didn't answer, she pulled out her cell and punched in his cell number.

"Hey, where are you?" she said when he answered. Loud music was blasting in the background and she could barely hear him.

"Ava?" Cliff yelled.

She used one finger to close her ear as she strained to hear. "Yeah, it's me. I can't hear you. Where are you?"

"I'm at the north pool!" he shouted. "It's loud out here. They have a big party going on, so I'll have to call you back later!"

The call was disconnected before Ava could say anything else. Ava slipped her cell into its compartment. After mulling over what to do next for a few moments, she decided just to walk across the property to the north pool. A party was definitely going on over there, so she might as well join Cliff.

Yet as she walked past the bar, she spotted two men salaciously leaning over her sister, who was swaying like she'd had too much to drink.

"So, what's your name again?" Mia asked, slurring her words.

"I'm Wham," the first guy said.

"And I'm Bam," the second guy replied.

Mia giggled. "Wham, Bam, thank you, ma'am."

They exchanged a sly glance. "How about we finish this conversation up in our room?" the first guy asked.

"How about you get lost?" Ava said, stepping into their conversation.

"Heeeey, sissy," Mia said, flapping her hand in a wave.

"What do you think you're doing?" Ava hissed.

"Just hanging with Wham and Bam. Or is it Bam and Wham?" she said, crossing her hands and pointing at the men. She cracked up laughing.

The men didn't see anything funny, though. "The lady's minding her own business. Why don't you go do the same, *Sissy?*"

"Sissy means sister. As in big sister. Which means I'm not going anywhere but off to call security if you don't get lost," Ava growled.

They gave her a fierce look, but she wasn't backing off.

"Come on, dude," the second guy said at last. "I don't need the drama. My wife will be back from her excursion soon."

The men shot Ava evil looks before walking away.

"Jerks," Ava mumbled.

"Hey, why did you run my friends off?"

"Come on," Ava said, grabbing her sister's arm. "I can't believe you're down here drunk at six o'clock in the evening."

"I'm not drunk," she protested. "Maybe a little tipsy." She smiled a big sloshy grin. "I told you, these piña coladas are serious."

"I'm taking you back to your room."

Mia took a deep breath and pulled herself together. "I'm fine," she said. "Maybe not well enough to drive, but since I'm not driving, that's not a problem." She started laughing again.

"Come on."

Mia jerked her arm away. "I am not going to my room. I'm vacationing in Aruba. So what if I'm a little tipsy? That's what you do in Aruba! Now, you can take that motherly act somewhere else. I'm about to have a good time." She brushed her dress down. "As a matter of fact, I'm about to go to a party over at the north pool. Everyone's talking about it."

Ava sighed heavily. She knew there was no

use trying to argue with her sister. She could be as stubborn as a mule. "Fine, I was about to head over to the north pool anyway. So, you'll come with me."

"Yay!" Mia clapped her hands. "I knew you had a little party girl in you! Let's go."

Ava and Mia arrived to find the party in full swing. Salsa music was blaring from the large speakers positioned all around the pool. A hotel employee was conducting a water game in the pool, and Ava spotted a limbo contest going on across the way. Ava glanced around for Cliff. She smiled when she spotted him going under the limbo pole. She watched as he successfully navigated his way under the pole without touching it. The man was a superb athlete, no doubt.

"Come on, there's Cliff," Ava said to her sister, who happily bounced off that way.

As they approached, Ava was about to tease him about his limbo performance when a short brunette jumped in front of her and threw her arms around his neck.

"Hey, Cliffffff," the woman squealed, dragging out his name. She had on a barely-there stars and stripes two-piece bikini. The top looked like it was struggling to contain her silicone breasts, and the bottom was nothing more than a G-string. But despite how trampy she looked, and the fact that she couldn't be any more than five feet two, Ava had to admit that she was one gorgeous woman.

"You did so good," the woman cooed to Cliff in a strong Latin accent. "And to think, you didn't want to limbo." The woman planted a kiss dead on Cliff's lips.

She wasn't letting go anytime soon, but Cliff had spotted Ava and gently pushed her off.

"Hey, Ava," he said, abashed. "Hi, Mia," he added. Mia waved but didn't respond.

"What's going on?" Cliff asked.

"Umm, nothing," Ava replied, looking at the woman, who was smiling widely at the two newcomers. She didn't let go of Cliff, however, but kept her arm draped through his. "Just checking to see what you were up to."

"Hi," the brunette said, waving. "I'm Sally."

"Hi, I'm Ava."

"Oh, you're Cliff's coworker."

Ava was shocked at the prickly feeling that was building in her body. She couldn't possibly be jealous, could she? What about dreamboat Julian?

"Yeah, I am the writer." She smiled meekly at Cliff.

Cliff looked uncomfortable. "Hey, Sally,

can you run and get us some drinks?" he finally said.

"Piña coladas?" she asked, her voice full of perkiness.

"Yes, and just bill it to my room."

"You got it, baby," she said before leaning in, kissing him lightly on the cheek, and strutting off.

"Well, well, well, Cliffy," Mia said, speaking up. "You found you a hot tamale, huh?"

"Yeah, look who's picking up strays now," Ava added, wondering how the woman knew his room number.

"Ha-ha, very funny," Cliff said. "No, Sally is a party animal and she's just showing me a good time."

"I bet she is," Ava said with a snort.

Both Cliff and Mia looked at Ava strangely. "Do I sense some hostility?" Cliff asked.

"Of course not, silly," Ava replied, feigning a smile. "I want you to enjoy yourself."

"He definitely seems to be doing that." Mia giggled.

"You were my inspiration," Cliff observed, ignoring Mia's comment. "I saw you getting your fling on and decided I needed to do the same. We can't come all the way to Aruba and not have some fun."

Ava folded her arms across her chest. "Julian is not a fling."

"Well, I'm not kidding myself. Sally *is* a fling." He leaned in and lowered his voice. "And the great thing is she doesn't mind being a fling."

Ava managed to laugh even though she didn't find his comment funny. She should have guessed that a world-traveling photographer knew his way around a hotel party.

Sally came bouncing back over, every curve on display for her new man. "Here, baby." She handed Cliff his drink. She turned to Ava and Mia. "Sorry, I didn't even think to ask you ladies if you wanted a drink."

"That *was* quite rude," Mia said.

"No, we're fine," Ava said, stepping in before her sister got out of line. "Well, I'm going to let you get back to, um . . ." She eyed Sally. "Your fun."

Sally giggled and grabbed Cliff's arm like she was staking her territory. "And boy, do I have some fun planned for you," she whispered loud enough for Ava to hear.

Cliff was embarrassed, and he told Ava, "We need to get together later so you can select the pictures to go with your story."

"Hopefully it will be much later," Sally said, pouting.

Ava faked a swooning-female smile. "Just

call me when you're done."

"Will do."

Ava reluctantly walked away, trying her best to tamp down the feeling of jealousy that was once again creeping up on her.

"So, you're just going to leave?" Mia asked, scurrying to catch up with her.

"What else am I supposed to do? He's enjoying himself."

Mia stopped her sister and spun her around. "Look, you can pretend all you want that you're interested in Julian, but that" — she pointed back toward Cliff — "is who you really want."

"I barely know him," Ava protested. "And you've seen Julian. That man is fine."

"And Cliff is no chop suey either. He's pretty fine himself."

That brought a smile to Ava's face. "He is fine, isn't he?"

"You can fight it," Mia said with a devilish smile, "but that chemistry between the two of you is undeniable. You want him. Even if you don't know you want him." She was delighted with this discovery. "I may be tipsy, but I can see that. So could Good-Time Sally. That's why she sank her claws into him."

Ava looked back over at Cliff. He was still watching her, even though Sally was dancing seductively in front of him. Was Mia right? Did she want him? The jealousy popping up inside her told Ava that her little sister just might be right.

19

Ava swirled her Moscato around in her wineglass. She and Cliff had met up a few hours later, chosen the photos to accompany her story, and headed down the street to a quaint little Italian restaurant for a late-night supper. Ava hadn't brought up Sally, but she was still wondering what had happened during those two hours.

"So, how was your date with Betty Boop?" Ava asked.

"Ha-ha-ha, very funny," Cliff replied. "May I ask, why do you care?"

Ava's hand went to her chest. "*Moi,* care? I'm here to have a good time, just like you. Have you forgotten the very fine, the very sexy Julian Lowe?"

Cliff quickly lost his smile. "I have to tell you, I don't trust that guy."

"Oh, now who's jealous?"

"Seriously, it's something about him."

"You don't even know him, so how can

you say you don't trust him?"

He waved his hand vaguely. "Whatever. I'm good at reading people, and if I feel something is wrong with someone, it generally is."

Ava had a suspicion she knew what was prompting that feeling, but she let it go. "Anyway, can we talk about something else? Tell me about you. Why are you single?"

"Oh, same old sad story. I'm the perfect *friend*," he said sarcastically. "Everyone always raves about what a wonderful *friend* I am."

Ava chuckled. "And I take it you don't like being friends."

"No, I love being friends," he said cheerfully. "In fact, I believe a couple should be friends first. You know, then grow into something else. I can just never seem to reach the 'growing into something else' phase." He chuckled and took a sip of his wine. "Women are always more turned on by men like my buddy Monty, who runs through women like an Olympic sprinter. And when those guys break women's hearts — which they always do — those women come cry on my shoulder." He stabbed the air in her direction. "But that's what you women want — the bad boy."

"No, that's what some women want," Ava

said, correcting him.

"Well, that's what all the women I've dealt with want."

"That's because you haven't found the right one yet. Who knows? Maybe Betty Boop is the right one," she said with a wicked smile.

"Again with the jokes."

Ava laughed as she sipped the last of her wine. She liked how calm she felt with Cliff. She could easily see how he could fall into the close-friend category. Cliff was strikingly handsome, so it seemed like any woman would love that about him. Shoot, her own sister had practically fallen all over him. Plus, he liked to get out and about. He was the type of guy who would do the limbo just for fun. Unlike Phillip, she thought, who could barely get off the couch.

"At the end of the day, I just want to be happy. I'm not getting any younger and I really am ready to settle down," Cliff noted. "I did have one good woman that I let get away," he said longingly, then shrugged off the memory. "But I was young, in the fraternity-boy party mode, and I messed up. Now she's happily married with two children and a dog, living the suburban life."

"Is that what you want?" Ava asked.

He seemed confused by the question.

Then he said, "I just want a life — outside of the *National Star.*"

"Why do you stay?" Ava asked gently. Cliff had told her he'd been at the *Star* for seven years. He usually landed the top assignments, like this one in Aruba. Still, he didn't seem like the tabloid type.

"Let's see," he replied, counting with his fingers, "six figures, with a six percent raise every year. You do the math."

"Yeah, I can't argue with that."

"Once you get past the chasing-celebrities part, it's really not a bad gig. You get to see the world on someone else's dime and make good money in the process. And I grew up poor," he added, tipping his glass toward her. "I have no desire to return to that lifestyle."

They laughed and talked some more before Ava finally stretched and said, "Well, I guess I should be getting back. I need to get to work on this story."

"Yeah, I'm kind of beat myself," Cliff said. He paid the bill and they made their way out onto the street. The bustling scene by day had seriously quieted down. "Do you want to catch a cab?" he asked.

"Let's walk. It's a beautiful night."

As they made their way down the sidewalk, Ava reflected on their evening. Despite all the flirtatious chemistry with Julian, tonight with Cliff had actually been her best night in Aruba. If she could always get matched up on assignments with him, the *Star* might not be all that bad.

20

Ava tossed and turned all night. The article was weighing heavily on her mind. She'd tried to write a story she knew would make Eli ecstatic, putting aside her conscience to write a scandal-plagued story, complete with details of Fredericko's threats.

But when she went to bed, India's words kept ringing in her head. She'd said, *If you get joy out of destroying people's lives, so be it.* Initially, Ava had been confident that she would do the job she'd come to Aruba to do, but the more she thought about ripping open these secrets, the more the story bothered her. She was so torn. Part of her wanted to do what she did best — report the stories people wanted to read. Not to mention impress the guys over at the television network by digging up a story no one else had. But the other part knew that India was right. What purpose would giving the *National Star* this story serve? A young singer's career would be destroyed, and it wasn't India's fault.

Ava finally pulled out her laptop. The sun was just rising and Ava hoped to churn out a brand-new story before her day got started.

She wiggled the mouse to take it off sleep mode, then waited as the screen popped up. Her article was still open. Ava stared at the headline. CON MAN, CRIMINAL . . . IS IT REALLY LOVE?

"That's so sensational," she muttered as she continued reading. *India Wright is known for her hit song "Love at Any Cost." Who knew that the megastar was talking about herself?*

Ava didn't bother reading the rest of the article. She knew what it said. She'd listed every piece of dirt that she'd dug up. She even wrote how India was well aware of Fredericko's sordid past, yet didn't care. The story gave her a sick feeling in the pit of her stomach. Usually, when she finished an article, the last sentence made her smile. That's because she'd always been proud of what she'd done, even those investigative pieces that had toppled big-time executives. But this article just made her ill.

Ava knew what she had to do. She opened a new blank document and began typing. Anyone lusting for scandal would have to read another article.

India Wright, poised and ready for the new chapter of her life, Ava typed. She proceeded to write a very neutral story. She detailed the wedding plans and India's passion for music. She did include the fact that India didn't have a prenup, just for a hint of drama, but she left it at that.

As Ava gave the story another read, she knew it was boring. Eli was not going to be pleased. It might even cost her the network job, but Ava simply couldn't ruin India. She didn't want that on her conscience.

Ava had just put the finishing touches on her new version when she heard a knock at her hotel room door. She looked out the peephole and was startled to see Julian.

"Hold on," she said, stepping into the bathroom to grab a robe. *What in the world is he doing here this early?*

"Hi," Ava said.

"Ummm, good morning." He eyed her bathrobe. "Is that the new breakfast attire?"

Ava grimaced. She'd been so caught up in this story, she'd forgotten about their breakfast date.

"I am so sorry." She pointed toward the laptop. "Duty calls."

"Are you up and working already?" he asked.

Ava nodded. "Yeah, I need to get this story turned in."

"Did you get everything you needed? Do you need me to fill in any information?" he asked. Ava thought it was sweet that he offered to fill in any holes, but she didn't want to get him in any trouble with India, so she demurred. "I got all that I need." She wondered if Julian knew what was going on. Come to think of it, maybe that was why he was here, to try to talk her out of filing the story.

Instead, Julian simply said, "Sooo, can we still do breakfast?"

Ava was mentally drained, but the mention of food set her stomach to growling.

"Sure, we can go eat. I'm starving." She glanced over at the laptop. "I just need to zap this story off to my editor."

"Well, I don't mind waiting," he said. "I'd love to catch the highlights on ESPN. I've been up working for a few hours myself, and my day just doesn't start right if I don't watch my ESPN."

Ava was hesitant, especially at the sight of Julian standing in her door in a silk button-down short-sleeved shirt, which was opened just enough to reveal a hint of his sexy chest. She shook off that thought. She wasn't going to jump his bones or anything. "Be my guest," Ava announced, stepping aside to let him in. "Just give me a minute."

He walked in, grabbed the remote, and plopped down on the sofa in front of the television. "Take your time," he said, turning the channel to ESPN. On the screen, a man was making chopping gestures as he spoke in a loud voice.

Ava walked back over to her laptop, typed a quick email to Eli, then attached her revised version. She felt good about her decision to redo the story, boring or not. Sure, this proved she wasn't cut out for this line of work, but that wasn't such a bad thing.

"Dang, this email is slow," Ava mumbled as she waited for the file to transmit.

"Probably because Aruba is for relaxation, not working. I'm sure high-speed Internet is not a top priority." Julian chuckled.

"Well, I'm going to get dressed while that's sending," Ava said, grabbing her clothes and darting into the bathroom.

Ten minutes later, Ava emerged wearing a comfortable maxi dress. She leaned over the desk, saw her file had been sent successfully, then shut off her computer.

"Are you ready?" she asked.

"And willing," he slyly said, standing up. As attracted as she was to him, his flirting didn't have nearly the same effect it had when they first met. Ava couldn't help but think Cliff had something to do with that.

21

Four hours after she'd had an enjoyable breakfast with Julian, Ava was on the hunt for her sister. Since she'd finished her story, maybe she and Mia could get in some relaxation. She'd called Mia's room and there was no answer. Her cell hadn't been on during the entire trip, and she didn't know the number to the BlackBerry Mr. Abernathy had given Mia, so Ava decided to just beat the pavement. Knowing Mia, she was probably lying out by the pool somewhere.

Downstairs, Ava spotted Mia holed up at a table in the hotel restaurant with Felix. She thought about leaving them to their privacy. After all, Felix was the type of positive influence that Mia needed in her life. But as she turned to head back to her room, an idea came to her. Maybe Felix could answer some questions she had. Her story was finished, so she wouldn't be violating his trust. Maybe he knew why no one could get through to India in regard to her prenup.

"Mind if I join you?" Ava said, approaching their table.

"Hey, sissy."

"Hey, Mia. Hi, Felix."

"Hello," Felix said. He looked annoyed that she'd interrupted them, but he covered that with a smile and said, "Of course you can join us." He stood up while Ava took a seat.

Ava watched in awe as Mia giggled, flirted, and acted like a giddy schoolgirl around Felix. Never in a million years would she have thought her sister would be attracted to a nerdy guy like him. But hey, she thought, maybe opposites do attract.

Ava ordered a light salad and a glass of iced tea, then joined in their conversation. Felix was meticulously outlining the ways wealthy people invest their money. Ava was dumbfounded at Mia's level of interest. She deduced that it must be because he was talking about money, her sister's favorite topic.

After they'd all finished eating, Felix asked, "So how'd your story about India turn out?"

"I turned it in this morning, so I'm just going to relax before I fly out day after tomorrow."

He nodded pensively and Ava decided to jump at her opening.

"So, Julian told me you were trying to encourage India to draw up a prenup."

He looked unsure of whether that was something he should be discussing.

"Well, uh . . ."

"Ava," Mia chastised, "don't ask him about his client's personal business."

Ava ignored her sister and leaned in. "Look, Felix, I'm not trying to get anything for my story. That story is done and on its way to the printer. I just don't understand how you guys could let her enter into a relationship that seems doomed from the start without encouraging her to protect herself."

"Ava . . ." Mia warned.

Felix held up his hand. "It's okay, Mia." He sighed heavily. "Between me and you, I don't understand it either," he told Ava. "India has always been so smart about her money. They could get married this week, he could divorce her next week, and he would be entitled to half her money." He shook his head and Ava could tell he'd worn himself out trying to talk to his client about this issue. "And especially with what I've found . . ." He immediately pressed his lips

159

together like he realized that he'd said too much.

"I'm sorry, I've said way more than I should have." He stood up. "Mia, as always it's been my sincerest pleasure."

"Where are you going?" Mia said, standing up as well.

"I told you that I have to go get some work done."

"Yeah, but I thought that wasn't until later."

Ava was shocked at how desperate her sister was acting. Could she really like him that much?

He smiled reassuringly. "Trust me, Miss Mia. You haven't seen the last of me. I actually want to go finish my business so I can take you out dancing this evening. I'll take care of the bill on my way out."

That promise brought a smile to Mia's face. "Then I'll see you tonight."

Felix leaned over and kissed her cheek. "Until then." He stepped back and nodded at Ava. "Good day, Miss Cole."

As soon as he was out of earshot, Mia spun on her sister. "Were you trying to run my date away on purpose?"

"I was not trying to run anyone away. I just asked a question."

Mia groaned. "You are so freaking nosy."

"I'm a reporter. I get paid to be nosy."

Mia slowly smiled. "Whatever. I'm in Aruba. I've met a nice man. I can't waste any negative energy fussing at you." She reached down to grab her purse. "Ta-ta, dear sister. I'm going to get some beauty rest before Felix takes me out on the town," she said, pushing back from the table.

Ava stood up with her. "So you like him, for real, for real?"

Mia clutched her purse to her chest and grinned widely. "I like him. For real. For real."

"Wow," Ava replied.

"And if things go the way I hope, I'll be making that trip to New York a lot more frequently." Mia waved and walked off, leaving her sister standing with her mouth gaping.

22

Cliff had an attitude with her and Ava didn't understand why. His lips were poked out, and he was answering all of her questions with terse one-word responses.

"Do you want to tell me what's the problem?" she finally asked. They were sitting at the hotel bar. He'd come downstairs shortly after Mia left, and she'd invited him over for a drink because she didn't feel like being stuck up in her room.

"I don't have a problem," he coolly responded.

"Cliff, the whole way you're saying you don't have a problem proves you have a problem."

He steadied his gaze on her. "Fine. I ran into your boyfriend on the way upstairs."

"Julian? First of all, he's not my boyfriend. Secondly, did he say something rude to you?"

"Yeah." Cliff hesitated. "Forget it, I don't

want to seem like some snitch."

"Cliff, what did he say?"

He really didn't want to say anything. Finally, he just blurted it out. "Well, I saw him all huddled up with that woman, India's assistant."

"What do you mean 'huddled up'?"

"Like he was all up in her face and they were whispering and stuff. It actually looked like they were arguing."

"And? They both work for India. Maybe they had a disagreement." Ava knew Cliff didn't care for Julian, but he was blowing things out of proportion.

"I didn't have a problem with them arguing, or even being huddled up. It was the way Julian reacted when he saw me. Like he was guilty of something. Then he had the nerve to tell me not to go starting drama with you when I didn't have a clue what was going on. Long story short, we exchanged a few sharp words and he told me I was just jealous because I wanted you."

Ava was taken aback. They were arguing over her?

"I made it clear we're just colleagues," Cliff clarified, "but I didn't appreciate the way he came at me. He's lucky I'm on the job or I would've punched him in the jaw."

Ava fought back an urge to smile. She

163

would bet Cliff had punched a few people in his time.

"What, you think that was funny?"

"No, no," she said, covering up quickly. "Don't let Julian get to you. You two probably just had a testosterone thing going."

"Maybe so." He laughed and finally relaxed. "Sorry for having a bad attitude. I guess I just don't like your boyfriend."

She swatted his shoulder. "Stop saying that. He's not my boyfriend."

"Oh, I'm sorry, your boy toy," he said jokingly.

"Oh, look who's talking. Like you and Sally just played Scrabble."

He chuckled. "And on that note, let's talk about something else. Did you get the story done and sent off?"

"I did," she said, grateful for the change in his mood, plus the change of subject. "I sent it off this morning, but I know Eli is not going to be too happy about it. I hadn't even called him about it because I didn't feel like getting chewed out."

That caused a genuine look of concern to pop up on Cliff's face. "What do you mean?"

She picked up her martini and took a sip. "It means I couldn't give up all the dirt on Fredericko, because I think it would ruin

India. I do believe he's crooked, but she's running scared and I just think this story would've exacerbated the problem." She shrugged. "I don't know. The whole celebrity peekaboo thing made me sick to my stomach."

Cliff stared blankly at her. "Wow. That's a first."

"What do you mean?"

"Well, I've been at the *Star* a long time, and you're the first reporter I've come across that has a conscience when it comes to filing a scandalous story."

She shrugged off his compliment. "That's just me. I don't get anything out of tearing someone else down."

"That's admirable," Cliff said. "What did Eli have to say about the story?"

Ava rubbed her temples. That was one conversation that she wasn't looking forward to. "I told you, I haven't heard from him yet. I thought he would've called to curse me out by now. I guess if I haven't heard from him by the time I get back to the room, I'll give him a call."

"So did the story end up being a fluff piece?"

"Basically. I watered down the drama and just focused on the wedding and her music. You know, the boring stuff."

Cliff leaned in and whispered, "Well, don't tell anybody but I think you did the right thing."

That perked up her spirits. He really was a good guy. "Thanks, I'm glad. I felt good about the decision. I just hope it doesn't cost me my job." She shrugged. "Although, honestly, I don't know if that would be a bad thing."

Cliff leaned back in his chair. "Don't feel bad. You have to be a special kind of person to be cut out for this line of work. I told you that on the plane ride over." He took a long swig of his imported beer. "The last reporter I was with, she disgusted me so much. You know she actually had sex with someone to get the story?"

"For real?" Ava was suddenly grateful she hadn't had sex with Julian. That would have been too much blurring of the lines.

"Yeah." He shook his head like the memory turned his stomach. "The people in this business can be ruthless, and they'll do whatever it takes to get the dirt."

"Well, that's not me."

"And I'm glad it's not," Cliff replied, eyeing her in a new light. "But I have to be honest, I don't know how long you'll be able to last at the *National Star* with that mentality."

"Well, hopefully I will have moved on before that becomes an issue. What about you? This job doesn't bother you?" He'd already told her he stayed in the job because of the money, but she really wanted to understand how he could do this every day and not let it bother him.

"Yeah, it does. I hate the jockeying for position to get the best photo, the million-dollar shot. But I've been lucky. I don't have to be out in the field with the hordes of photographers running down the street after Britney Spears's car. I usually get sent out on assignments with people who have agreed to talk to us, so I'm not fighting to get the best shot." He didn't seem entirely satisfied with that answer, and he added, "But I'm working toward a goal myself. Saving my money."

"Oh, really?"

He nodded like the thought of whatever he was saving for brought him internal joy. "Yeah, I'm not trying to do this for the rest of my life. I'm saving my money to start my own photography studio. That's where I plan to launch my exhibit. I have another year, max, then I should have enough to branch out on my own."

"In this climate? You don't think you'll have any problems?"

He grinned confidently. "You saw my work. But when we get back you'll have to let me come over and take your picture. I do some great alter-ego photos."

"Wow. What would be my alter ego?" She didn't miss how he eased an invitation in there. She wasn't offended, though. She actually thought it was nice.

Cliff leaned back and studied her for a moment. "Seems to me like you got this good girl/bad girl thing going," he finally said.

She laughed. If only he knew, he'd hit the nail on the head. The good girl was the one who had stuck with Phillip all this time, who refused to step outside her relationship. Even though she'd been approached by many men, even though she'd been tempted, and as miserable as she was, she never cheated on him. The bad girl was the one who now wanted to rip a man's clothes off, present company included.

"Well, if you'll excuse me for a minute, I'm going to run to the restroom." He pushed back from the bar and stood up. "All these drinks are taking their toll. Keep my seat warm."

"Will do." Ava sipped her drink as he disappeared around the corner. She glanced down at her watch. She hadn't even realized that they'd been sitting at the bar talking for over two hours.

"I guess you want to learn the hard way," a man leaning in from behind her whispered.

Ava spun on her bar stool to come face-to-face with Fredericko. He was wearing dark shades, but there was no mistaking his firm jawline and smooth skin. He had on a pair of neatly starched slacks, a white silk shirt, and a brown camel-hair jacket. As usual, he looked like he had just stepped off the pages of *GQ*.

"I warned you, stay out of my business," he growled.

She tried to steady her hand, which was nervously twitching. This man creeped her out. She could see why people in his old neighborhood were frightened by him. "And I told you that I don't scare that easily."

"You're a smart-ass, aren't you?"

"Shouldn't you be somewhere getting ready for your wedding?"

He ignored her question, firing back one of his own. "You think you know it all, don't you?"

"No, I don't. Just digging up what I can," she replied calmly.

He looked at her with disdain. "I can't wait."

"You can't wait for what?"

A wicked grin spread across his face. "The truth. We'll see how smug you are when the truth comes out."

"What are you talking about?" she said, maintaining her cool. "Why don't you enlighten me with the truth?" She said a silent prayer that Cliff would hurry up and return from the restroom.

"For the last time, mind your own business and stay out of mine," Fredericko threatened.

It was Ava's turn to lean in toward him. "She's still marrying you," she whispered. "Despite the fact that we all know you're hiding something, but it's her call, not mine."

Hatred filled his eyes as he glared at her. "Again, let the record reflect, you ruin me, I ruin her *and you.*"

"Again, let the record reflect that you don't scare me," Ava said, even though he did.

"You have no idea who you're messing with."

"Once again, is that a threat? Because if it is, I'd love for that to be the headline in next week's magazine."

In a show of defiance, Fredericko had the audacity to pick up her drink and take a sip. "So pretty, yet so foolish." He set her drink down, popped the olive in his mouth, then turned and stormed off. Ava shuddered as he walked away. She pushed her tainted drink toward the edge of the bar. "Bartender," she called out, "can you fix me another drink? And make it a double."

She would not let herself be bullied. Yet his threatening behavior truly frightened her, especially since she knew he could back up what he said. She would have to watch her step from now on.

"Hey, I'm back," Cliff said, sitting down. "Say, what's wrong? You look like someone just said they wanted to kill you."

He didn't say it, Ava thought, *but there was no doubt — Fredericko definitely wanted her dead.*

23

Ava made her way down to the lobby, where she was meeting Julian to go sightseeing around the island. She smiled when she saw him standing near the front desk in a pair of Bermuda shorts and a tight white Nike T-shirt. He was turning the heads of quite a few women in the room, and she felt good knowing that he was going out with her.

"I hope I didn't keep you waiting too long," she said as she approached. "My sister was up in my room, ransacking my stuff. Felix is taking her sightseeing on the island today, too."

"No, you're fine," Julian said. "You know, Felix worked all night so he could spend the day with her. I guess she's done something to him. Well, are you ready to go?"

Ava nodded. She couldn't wait to ask him about what Fredericko had said. Maybe he could shed some light on what she would "soon see."

"I'm looking forward to finally having some fun," Julian said. "Let me get that."

He was reaching for her beach bag when they heard someone scream.

"You bitch!" They both turned to see a raging India charging toward them. Felix was close behind her.

The commotion caught Ava completely off guard and she stood frozen as India lunged at her. Thankfully, Julian grabbed India before her fingernails could make contact.

"India, what is wrong with you?" Julian asked as he struggled to hold her back.

India's face was streaked with mascara. She had on a silk robe and her hair was still pinned up in rollers, like she'd been in the middle of a makeup session.

"Why did you come down here with no clothes on?" Julian asked, trying to shake her to calm her down. "Felix, what's going on?"

"I don't know. We were meeting, she got a fax, and she just stormed out," he said, frazzled himself.

India struggled to break free. "That bitch is what's wrong!" she yelled as she took a swing at Ava.

"What did I do?" Ava cried, taking a step back out of her reach.

"What did you do?" India repeated. "What did you do? You know what you did and I hope you're happy."

"India . . ." Julian looked around nervously. Several people had stopped and were staring at the unfolding spectacle. "I need you to pull it together," he said, lowering his voice.

"Pull it together? How am I supposed to pull it together?" she cried. "Have you seen this?" India waved a piece of paper in his face.

"What is it?" Julian asked as he took the paper from her.

"It's only my life ruined," she yelled at Ava.

What in the world is on that paper? Ava wondered. "India, I really don't know what you're talking about."

"Shut up, you lying tramp!" India screamed. Before Ava could react, India reached around Julian's shoulder and slapped Ava so hard it left her cheek stinging.

"India!" Julian grabbed India and pushed her back against a wall. He started whispering something. Ava couldn't make out what he was saying, but it was obviously calming her down.

"Michael, where's Jackie?" Julian said to

174

India's bodyguard, who had just appeared by India's side and was also trying to calm her.

"I don't know, Mr. Lowe. She was in her suite last I checked," the burly man responded.

"Find her! Get her to help calm India down." Julian turned his attention back to India. "India, remember where you are. You're here for a wedding, so people are watching you. You need to pull it together."

"There's not going to be a wedding," India spat. "Fredericko called it off because of her." She pointed at Ava.

Ava didn't think that was bad news, but she was still wondering what that had to do with her.

"You've ruined our lives!" India snatched the paper out of Julian's hand and shook it at Ava again. "Because of this. Someone faxed it to me this morning. And by now every media outlet in the country will be digging in our business. I'll be the laughing-stock of the entertainment industry. It's over! My career, everything is over!" She flung the paper at Ava.

Ava stared at the paper that had landed at her feet. She leaned down to pick it up. CON MAN AND CRIMINAL . . . IS IT REALLY LOVE? Ava read. On the paper was a copy of the front page of the *National Star.* She looked up in disbelief. "India, I . . ."

"You what? You're a low-down, dirty, funky tabloid reporter who has no life of her own and gets her jollies destroying other people's lives. I hope you're happy. The magazine has hit the stands, and everyone in New York is talking about it." Her body shook as she broke down sobbing. "My life is ruined." She glared at Ava. "All because of you."

"Michael, get her out of here!" Julian said.

"It's not like that. I can explain . . ." Ava said as Michael led India off. She really couldn't, though. She couldn't explain anything because she herself couldn't understand how in the world the wrong story had ended up on the cover of the *National Star.*

"Who sent that fax?" Julian asked Felix, who was looking distressed.

"I . . . I don't know," he stammered. "So much is happening." He looked around nervously. "I need to speak with you privately. I hacked into a few protected files and found some things that don't add up. That's what I was reviewing with India. It's pretty bad."

Julian sighed heavily, then turned to Ava. "I'm sorry. I need to handle this."

Ava nodded. "Okay. But, Julian, I don't know what happened. Really, I —"

He held up his hand to cut her off. "Just give me some time to work all of this out, okay?" he said wearily. "I'll call you later."

Ava sighed in frustration as he took off after India. She read the paper again. That was definitely her article. She couldn't believe she'd messed up that bad and sent Eli the wrong story. How had her trying to do the right thing ended so horribly?

24

Ava was barely inside her room before she dialed the office. She anxiously waited as Eli's secretary tracked him down.

"Ava!" Eli exclaimed when he finally came to the phone. "How's my superstar reporter doing? Girl, you know how to come in with a bang. I knew there was a reason we brought you on board." He sounded absolutely ecstatic.

"Eli, that's not the story I sent," Ava cried. She'd racked her brain trying to figure out how she'd messed up and sent the wrong story. She had purposefully named the two files something different.

"What do you mean it's not the one you sent? Yes it is. And a damn good story at that," he replied. "I had them stop the presses and put this story in instead. You outdid yourself."

"Eli —"

"Look, I want you to try and see if you

can get India's reaction to the story," he continued, not giving her a chance to get a word in edgewise. "See what she has to say. Find out, is the wedding still on? You know how to do it."

"There isn't going to be a wedding! Fredericko called it off!" Ava shouted.

"What? Hot diggity dog!" Eli raved. "All right, we'll run that as the lead story in the next issue. I'll get someone to see what we can dig up here."

"Eli!" she said, cutting him off. "I don't know what's going on. I sent a different story."

"Yeah, I know. You sent two stories. The first was some old boring fluff piece and I don't do fluff," he said with an edge. "I don't even know why you wasted your time with that one. I was just about to call you out on it when I read this second one. Oh boy, you sure made up for it with that one. Of course, I had to spice it up, give it that *National Star* touch."

"I don't understand," Ava said. Had she mistakenly attached both stories? She opened her computer to log on and check her sent mail folder.

"Nothing to understand," he said. "Damn good job, Cole. I know your flight comes back tomorrow, but if you need more time, you say the word, we'll keep you there."

"But, Eli —"

"Gotta go. The big guy upstairs is so pleased with this story that he wants to meet on it. He hardly ever gives his input to the editorial department, so this is major." Eli's excitement radiated through the phone. "The magazine is flying off the shelves already, all the entertainment shows are talking about it, and we've had so many hits to the website that it crashed. You are a winner, girl. Call me when you get something else." He hung up the phone before she could get another word in.

Ava was stunned. How in the world had this mix-up happened? She just couldn't understand how she could make a mistake like this. She'd ruined India's life. And for what? A paycheck?

Ava's thoughts were interrupted by a knock on the door. She started not to answer it, but then she heard Cliff say through the door, "Ava, are you all right?"

She walked over and slowly opened the door.

"Why are you crying?" Cliff said, gently touching her cheek. She hadn't even realized she'd been crying. But as she put her hands up to her face, she noticed her wet cheeks. "Everyone is buzzing about what just happened. I don't mean to intrude, but, well, I was worried about you. You know, since you told me how you felt about bringing India down, I was a little shocked to find that you did the story anyway."

"That's just it, I didn't," Ava said, turning to walk back into the room. Cliff followed.

"What are you talking about?"

"I mean, I did do the story." She walked back over to the laptop. "But I had a change of heart and I wrote a different story." Her computer was on now, so she logged on to her email account. She immediately noticed an email from Felix. Why would India's accountant be emailing her? She quickly opened it. *Need to talk to you. Got something you might be interested in. Call me asap. Room 1613.*

She wondered what he wanted. She closed the email and went to her sent folder. She'd deal with Felix later. Right now she had to find out what was going on with her story.

Cliff came up behind her and stood over her shoulder. "What are you doing?"

Ava's heart sank when she saw her email to Eli, along with both stories attached. Ava slowly turned to Cliff. "I sent both," she said softly. "I sent both stories and ruined this woman's life." Ava sank into Cliff's arms in tears.

25

Ava couldn't believe Julian had showed up at her door. After the bombshell that had been dropped this morning, she thought he wouldn't have two words for her.

"How are you?" he asked after Ava had opened her hotel door.

"I've seen better days," Ava replied. She looked back at Cliff, who was sitting in the chair at the desk. He'd stayed with her most of the afternoon. She'd stopped crying about an hour ago, thanks to Cliff, who was cracking jokes and had her feeling a whole lot better.

Julian peered over Ava's shoulder. "Umm, is this a bad time?"

Ava didn't know what to say. She didn't want to kick Cliff out, but she really wanted to explain to Julian that she hadn't meant to turn in the first story. He had to be upset with her, and she just wanted the chance to tell him what had happened.

"I guess that's my cue," Cliff said dryly. He stood and made his way toward the door.

"I'll call you later," Ava said as Cliff walked out.

He just grunted and didn't respond. Ava wasn't sure, but she thought she saw Julian smirk.

"Come on in," Ava said after Cliff was gone.

"So, are you okay?" Julian asked after they got settled on the balcony.

Ava leaned back in the wicker patio chair. "I'm fine, I guess. I'm ready to get home. My editor was thrilled about the story, so I'm in his good graces." She looked Julian in the eye. "But I need you to know, that's not the story I intended to send. I wrote two versions and somehow I attached both," she explained. "I understand if you're furious, because I know India is a good friend and client. And I know this will probably just bring unnecessary attention and drama to you guys. That was not my intent."

Julian held up his hand to cut her off. "No need to explain. I told you, I understand you were just doing your job. I was a little shocked by everything you dug up, and the fact that India knew about it all . . ." He shook his head. "Of course, I'm concerned for India, but believe it or not, my life doesn't revolve around her. I do have my own life and you've made me realize that I need to take more time out for me. Since there isn't going to be a wedding now, and after the stressful day we've all had, I just wanted to make good on my rain check."

Ava felt relief wash through her body. She couldn't believe he wasn't furious with her.

"So, you still want to spend time with me?"

Julian looked at her solemnly. "We're both leaving tomorrow. Your sister has gone out with Felix. India just wants to be alone. We might as well try to enjoy ourselves."

Ava couldn't help it, she fell into his embrace. Julian hugged her tightly for a few minutes. "You are so beautiful, do you know that?" he asked as he released her.

Ava gently smiled as she tried to remember the last time anyone had said those words to her. Certainly not Phillip. She couldn't remember the last time he'd said anything sweet or vaguely romantic to her.

"Let's go take a walk," Julian said. "I don't know about you, but I could use some fresh air. This has been some kind of day."

That sounded like a good idea to Ava. She was past ready to go home and put this nightmare of a trip behind her. But getting out and enjoying the fresh Aruba night air might be just what she needed.

Julian led the way as they began their stroll outside the hotel. He didn't bring up India; instead he asked Ava more questions about her past and her home life.

After twenty minutes, Julian suggested they take a side street and head down toward a secluded spot on the beach. That sounded fine to Ava. She wondered what he would do when they were alone.

They'd just turned on the street when someone yelled, "Give me your money!"

Ava stopped in her tracks at the sight of the two menacing men standing in front of her. One had to be at least six feet tall. The other was no more than five five. Both of them wore dark gray shirts and jeans.

"Excuse me?" she said.

"You speak English? Give me your money," one of the guys said as he reached for the strap of her Coach purse draped across her body.

"Hey, are you crazy?" Julian said, coming to her defense.

The taller of the two guys roughly pushed him to the ground. "Say, man, ain't nobody talking to you. I'm talking to the pretty lady here."

As Julian scrambled to get up off the

ground, the short guy landed a swift kick to his side. Julian groaned as the tall guy screamed at Ava. "I said, give me the purse," the guy said, snatching Ava's bag. Instinct made Ava want to snatch the purse back, but the look on the man's face let her know that these guys would kill her if she created any trouble.

The man who had kicked Julian walked around the back of her. "Umph, you sure are a sweet thing."

Ava was terrified as his eyes roved up and down her body. He looked like a hungry wolf about to attack its prey.

"You've got the purse, just go and leave us alone," she said, her voice quavering.

"Yeah," Julian added, pulling himself up.

The guy who had taken the purse dropped it, then pulled out a switchblade. Before Ava could flinch, he grabbed her and held the knife to her throat. "Maybe I want more than a purse." He laughed.

Tears started flowing down Ava's face. Fear gripped her. Would she ever see her family again? Would the last thing people remembered about her be that she helped bring down a pop star?

"Let her go!" Julian said, taking a step toward them.

The guy pulled Ava closer and she let out

a scream. "Don't make me cut her!" he yelled.

The other guy stepped up to Julian and popped out a knife as well. "Unless you want to get cut, too, I suggest you get lost."

"I'm not going anywhere," Julian said firmly.

The guy stepped closer and began waving the knife. "You're what?"

Julian looked at Ava in fear, then back at the man. He eased back a step.

Is he about to run? Ava wondered.

"If you know what's good for you, you'll get out of here," the short guy said.

Julian continued looking back and forth. Finally he said, "I'm . . . I'm going to go get help." He turned and took off. Ava's eyes bucked in disbelief.

The man who was holding Ava pulled her forward. "Come on," he said, dragging her toward an alley. Ava was scared out of her mind as images of being raped raced through her mind. Would they kill her and dump her body? Would she never be found, like Natalee Holloway?

Ava couldn't believe this. The fact that Julian had left her alone turned her stomach. How could he do that? Despite her disgust, she had bigger worries at the moment. Was Fredericko making good on his threat?

"So, you wanna see Aruba," one of the men spat while the other one held her down. "I'll give you something to see, all right." He held the knife firmly in one hand while he used his other hand to unbutton his jeans. Ava screamed, but it was quickly cut off as the man holding her stuffed a piece of cloth into her mouth and used another piece of material to tie her arms up. Then he roughly straddled her.

Ava's eyes were blinded by tears as she fought to get the man off her. She thrashed madly from side to side. They were laughing as if her fear only turned them on more. Ava finally grew weary under his weight. She fell limp after several minutes of kicking. There was no way she could overpower the two of them. She could only hope that if this was to be her fate, death would come quickly.

"Hey! Who's in there!" Ava felt her heart jump as a bright light flashed toward them.

Both men snapped their heads toward the light.

"What are you doing down there? I'm a security guard! I've already called the police!" he called out.

Ava didn't know who had come to her rescue and she didn't care. All that mattered was that her attackers had stopped.

The second of confusion was enough for her to act. She kneed the man holding her down in the groin, and when he doubled over in pain, she jumped up and took off running toward the light.

She collapsed into the stranger's arms.

Ava's attackers must have decided they needed to get away while they still could because they took off in the opposite direction.

"Are you okay?" the stranger, an elderly security guard, asked as he untied her hands and removed the cloth from her mouth.

Ava breathed a sigh of relief as she hugged the man. "I . . . I'm okay now. Thank you so much."

"Well, they're gone. You're gonna be fine." He flashed his light on her to examine her for any cuts or bruises. "You're bleeding on your arm, but it doesn't look major. Still, I say we get you to a hospital."

The stranger started leading her toward a nearby store. "We'll go in here and call for help." He looked at her sadly as he walked her across the street. "What is a woman like you doing out here alone?"

She wanted to scream, *I wasn't alone. That bastard left me.* But the only thing she could find the strength to say was, "Cliff, I need to call Cliff."

"Okay, okay," the man said. "We'll get you to a hospital, then we'll find this Cliff person, okay?"

Ava tightly clutched his arm as the security guard led her inside to call for help.

26

"You are one lucky lady," said the young doctor standing over Ava.

Ava rubbed her temple. She was sitting up in a cot in a dingy hospital room. The place was a far cry from the state-of-the-art facilities she was used to back in the States.

Ava glanced over at the clock on the wall. It was two in the morning.

"So, I can go?" she asked the doctor. They'd wrapped her upper arm in a bandage because it had been scraped, probably when her attackers had dragged her. But other than that, she didn't appear to have any major damage.

"Are you sure you're okay?" Cliff said. "I don't think you should be leaving."

Ava didn't remember when he'd arrived. The last thing she remembered was riding in the car to the hospital with the security guard who'd saved her. She did remember giving him Cliff's cell number and the name of the hotel.

"It really is okay for her to go," the doctor said.

"I'm fine," Ava said, wanting to leave this place.

"You may be sore for a couple of days. I have a prescription for you. You should be able to get it filled at our pharmacy downstairs." The doctor turned to Cliff. "Are you her husband?"

Cliff shook his head. "No, we work together."

"Well, your colleague is truly one of the lucky ones. This could've turned out a lot differently if she hadn't escaped. These random acts can sometimes have disastrous results."

Ava made a mental note to send something special to the security guard when she returned home.

"Where is the police station so we can go file a report?" Cliff asked.

The doctor released a small laugh. "Oh, I wouldn't count on anything being done about this. She's walking away, so as far as the police will be concerned, there was no harm done. They don't like anything to tarnish our perfect tourist image. They've been struggling to rebuild since that American girl disappeared, so they won't give any credence to this. I can tell you now, they'll say it was just a random occurrence."

"This wasn't random," Cliff said forcefully.

The doctor tore off the prescription he'd just written and handed it to Cliff. "If it wasn't, then I'll say you're extremely lucky." He smiled reassuringly before exiting the room.

Cliff helped Ava off the hospital bed and out to the waiting cab. He rode with her back to the hotel, then situated her in her room.

"Have you heard from my sister?" Ava asked.

"I left a message on her room phone when I was heading to the hospital. I guess she's still out with Felix."

"Well, I think we should definitely talk to him. He sent me that email, so maybe it had something to do with this," Ava said once she'd gotten settled in her bed. "And we should try to find out if Fredericko is still on the island, see if we can track him down, because I know he was behind my attack. We should go tomorrow and try to talk to India again to see if she knows anything about the people who attacked me."

Cliff looked at her like she'd lost her

mind. "What? You've done your story. And if Fredericko is behind this, that's even more reason to leave it alone. You already got what you need. I know you're not thinking of writing more."

"Of course I am. Why wouldn't I?" She still hadn't told him about the job offer with the network, but now, more than ever, she had something to prove.

"Ummm, because someone just tried to kill you!"

"Which means that they're scared of me discovering something really major." She grimaced as she tried to get comfortable.

"This is ridiculous," Cliff said. "It's time for us to go. You've got your story, so let's get out of here. I'm trying to figure out how we can move our flight up."

Ava was firm in her conviction to stay. "I can't leave until I get some answers. Eli said I could extend my time if I was on to something, and I'm definitely on to something."

He continued to stare at her in disbelief. "Is this story worth your life? You were just attacked by two thugs. They were probably going to kill you. I guess you're not going to be happy until they succeed."

She shivered at the memory of those rough hands holding her. "Whatever.

They're not going to scare me off. They can't intimidate me into not following this story."

Cliff shook his head in exasperation. "You know what? You are so blind. You can't see the danger around you and you can't see . . ."

"And I can't see what?"

"You know what? Just forget it! It's not like you'll listen to me anyway. But you keep trying to bring some serious journalism to the National Star if you want. It's not going to make a difference. I've been there seven years and I know what they care about. The story and that's it. If you get killed trying to gather a story for them, they'll send flowers to your funeral, then send another reporter to finish the story without thinking twice." Cliff was so angry, and Ava couldn't understand why he was overreacting.

He took a deep breath. "Just take these pain pills and get some rest," he said, handing her two large pills. "I'm going to stay here until you fall asleep. Just to make sure you're okay."

Ava couldn't help but smile. As angry as he was, he still wasn't going anywhere. Ava popped the pills in her mouth, swallowed the cup of water he handed her, then lay

back and relished the sleep that overtook
her.

27

Ava squinted to make out where she was. It took a minute to register that she was in her hotel room, tucked beneath the goose-down comforter.

She glanced over and saw Cliff sleeping in the chair by the window. "Hey," Ava said, sitting up.

Cliff stirred to attention. "Are you all right?"

She nodded, then yawned. "How long have I been out?"

"You slept awhile, twelve hours. I guess it's the medicine. How do you feel?"

Suddenly, everything came back to her and she remembered the attack. "I'm fine," she said timidly. "I guess it could've been a whole lot worse."

"Well, the doctor said, with the exception of your soreness, you got a clean bill of health."

"Have you heard from . . . ?" Ava caught herself.

"Your boyfriend? No. I haven't seen the jerk and you'd better hope I don't see him either." The fire burning in his eyes reminded Ava that she'd told Cliff all the details about the attack — including Julian taking off. She couldn't wait to hear the explanation he had for that.

"I actually was going to say Mia," Ava lied. She didn't want to get Cliff worked up.

Cliff relaxed a little. "She's already been over twice. She came by last night right after you dozed off, then again this morning. She's worried because she can't hook up with Felix. That's what she was doing when we returned last night, walking around asking people if they'd seen him."

"Where is he?" Ava hoped that her sister hadn't had sex with Felix and then he'd pulled a disappearing act.

Cliff shrugged. "Frankly, I don't care about seeing any of them again. I just want to leave this place. Your sister was on the flight this morning, but she changed it to fly out with us this evening. She wanted to make sure you were okay."

Ava threw the covers back. "She didn't have to do that," she said, reaching for the phone. "Let me call and tell her I'm up."

As soon as Mia heard Ava's voice, she dropped the phone. A few seconds later, she was banging on Ava's hotel door.

Cliff opened the door and Mia nearly knocked him over as she raced inside. "Oh, my God. I was so worried." Mia threw her arms around her sister's neck. "I thought you were in a coma!"

Cliff made a face. "I tried to tell her it wasn't that serious."

"But you wouldn't wake up!"

"It was the painkillers," Cliff said.

Mia stepped back and looked her sister up and down. "Are you sure you're all right?"

Ava nodded. "I don't even have much of a headache anymore."

"Well, can you fill me in on what happened? Cliff says he got a call that you'd been attacked. He went and picked you up at the hospital. All he kept saying was it was Julian's fault."

Ava let out a heavy sigh. Cliff didn't manage to hide his disgust.

"Well, if you're sure you're fine, I'm going to go pack my bags," he said, heading toward the door.

"I am fine. I need to pack myself," Ava said, looking around the hotel room at her belongings strewn everywhere.

Cliff looked lovingly at her and Ava felt a warmth fill her heart. "Just ring if you need anything. I'll be back in about an hour."

"Go," Mia shooed him. "I can take care of my sister."

When he was gone, Ava pulled herself out of bed. "Let me pack my stuff."

"Are you sure you can do this?"

"Girl, I'm fine. Who's acting like the mom now?"

Mia touched her sister's arm and said softly, "Is it true that Julian took off and left you?"

Ava nodded, still wishing there was some kind of explanation. "He said he was going for help."

"That is so lame." Mia paused. "Unless . . . do you think something might have happened to him? Maybe he's with Felix."

"That's right. Cliff said you can't find Felix."

"I can't, which is very strange. I mean, he acted so into me. We had such a great time dancing the other night, then we spent all day yesterday sightseeing. He walked me to my room yesterday and was supposed to come back to take me to dinner, and I haven't talked to him since. Every night since we've met, he's called to say good night and he didn't last night."

She sounded genuinely worried. For her part, Ava was relieved to hear that they hadn't spent the night together.

"So you really like this guy?" Ava asked.

"I do." Mia plopped down on the bed. "Can you believe it? He's such a nerd. But in a cute way." She smiled slyly. "And he's rich."

Ava chuckled. "So you like him because he's rich?"

"No, because he's not like Jay-Z rich. He's like work-hard-for-my-money rich. And I like knowing that I'm the best thing that's ever happened to him."

"And how did you come to that conclusion?"

She shrugged. "I don't know. I can just tell. Regardless, I'm looking forward to seeing where it goes. And I know he was, too, which is why I don't understand why he just up and disappe . . ." Her words trailed off as she glanced over at the nightstand. She jumped up and grabbed the multicolored oversize handkerchief. "Where'd you get this?" she asked, her eyes wide.

Ava looked at the handkerchief, confusion blanketing her face. Then she remembered. "That's what those goons used to tie my hands. I held onto it because I wanted to report it to the police, but the doctor said we shouldn't even bother. Why?"

Mia's eyes met Ava's. "This is Felix's handkerchief," she slowly said.

"What?" The coincidence was too great for Ava to believe it. "Maybe it's one that just looks like one he has."

Mia shook her head. "No, it's vintage Burberry. They haven't made one of these in years. I complimented him on it when we went dancing. He found this in London." She examined the handkerchief, turning it over. "Oh, my God." She pointed to the corner. In small stitching were the initials FJS.

Ava's hand went to her mouth. Before she could say anything, Mia was headed toward the door.

"Where are you going?" Ava asked, following her.

"I'm going to his room. I didn't go last night because I was scared that, well, I thought maybe he'd met someone else. But no, something is definitely wrong. I have to go check on him. And if he doesn't answer, I'm going to call hotel security."

"Mia, maybe we should call security first," Ava said. But Mia didn't listen. She burst into the hallway and hurried off. Ava grabbed a sundress to throw over her gown as she followed her sister out.

"What floor is he on?" Ava asked.

"The sixteenth floor," Mia said, not losing her stride.

Ava had to stop and catch her breath by the time they made it to Felix's floor. Mia was already down the hall. She stopped in front of Felix's door.

"Felix," Mia yelled, banging on the door. "Felix, it's Mia, open up!"

She waited anxiously, yet heard nothing.

Ava caught up to her sister and grabbed her arm. "Mia, let's call security."

"Felix, it's me, Mia," she called out again.

"Come on," Ava said, pulling at her.

Mia snatched her arm away. "No, something is wrong." She looked up and down the hallway and noticed the housekeeper wheeling her cart into a room a few doors down.

"Excuse me!" Mia said, racing over to her. "I need to get into this room. It's an emergency."

The woman looked at Mia like she didn't understand.

"That room, right there," Mia said, pointing to Felix's room. "I need you to let me in."

"No, no. I no do that," the woman said.

"Mia, let's call security," Ava repeated.

Mia eyed the housekeeper again. "Lady,

this is an emergency."

"No, no. I no do that," the woman said again.

"Uggh," Mia said, reaching out and yanking the woman's master key out of her hand and darting back down the hall to Felix's room.

"Hey!" the woman called out. Before the housekeeper could reach Mia, she had the key in the door and was entering Felix's room.

Ava was following her sister through the door when Mia let out a bloodcurling scream. Ava stepped inside and saw what had Mia about to lose her mind. Felix was laid out across the bed, and the white plush comforter was covered in blood. One prominent bullet hole filled the middle of his forehead.

"Oh, my God!" Ava said, pulling her sister's arm. "Let's get out of here."

Mia just stood there, trembling and crying.

"Come on." She literally dragged Mia out as the housekeeper also started screaming. They raced to the end of the hall, picked up the house phone, and called for help.

"We're on the sixteenth floor. There's a man. He's dead in room sixteen thirteen," Ava panted into the phone.

"Is he breathing?" the person on the other end asked.

"I don't know. Just come!"

It seemed like forever, but in actuality five minutes later Felix's room was buzzing with police officers and hotel management. Other hotel guests had begun sticking their heads out of their doors, trying to see what was going on. Mia was still shaking uncontrollably. A policeman walked over. "I need to question you two. Can you tell us what you saw?"

"Well, my sister is the one who found him."

The officer turned to Mia. "Ma'am, can you tell us what you saw?"

"I . . . I . . . Oh, my God. He's dead."

"Ma'am, I know this is difficult, but I need you to calm down and talk to me," the officer said.

Mia tried to calm herself down. She took a deep breath and said, "I just walked in and saw him there. He was like that, laid out. Blood was everywhere." Mia buried her head in her sister's shoulder and sobbed.

"How you see him is how we found him," Ava said, rubbing Mia's back. "We don't know anything more than that."

The officer took down some notes, including their names and numbers.

"Can we go back to our rooms?" Ava asked the officer. "My sister is kinda losing it."

The officer nodded as he looked down at his notepad. "I have your room numbers here, right?" He glanced back up at them. "You're free to go. Just please don't leave the property until the detective gets here. He's on his way."

Ava escorted her sister back to her room. After some coaxing and a shot of rum, Mia calmed down. By that time Cliff had arrived.

"How is she?" Cliff asked after Ava filled him in on everything.

"Still shaken up." Mia was laid out across the bed, a wet rag across her eyes.

"Let's step outside," Ava said. "Mia, sweetie, I'll be right back."

Mia didn't respond as Ava and Cliff stepped out into the hallway.

"This is wild," Cliff said. "Do they know what happened?"

"No, they don't," Ava said. "We went upstairs and found him there." Ava then pulled the handkerchief out of her pocket and filled Cliff in on that part of the story.

"This story just keeps getting stranger by the moment," he said when she was finished. "And more dangerous by the moment. I'm just glad we're leaving today."

They stopped talking as Mia opened the door and poked her head out.

"Hey, are you okay?" Ava asked.

Mia sniffed as she walked into Ava's arms. "I wanna go home."

Ava held her sister as she cried and mumbled, "I wanna go home, too."

28

Ava finally persuaded Mia to let go by convincing her she needed to go pack. Their flight left in four hours, and that's all Mia needed reminding of. She was so ready to leave Aruba.

Ava had just returned to her room when Cliff met her at the door.

"Look, I was thinking, you said there was a detective they wanted you to talk to?" he said.

Ava nodded. "Yeah, they asked us not to leave until he had a chance to interview us."

"So, do you think the people that attacked you also killed Felix?"

"It looks that way."

Cliff studied the handkerchief like he was trying to figure out his next move. "Come on. Let's go see this detective."

Ava didn't ask any questions as she followed him upstairs.

"We need to speak to the detective in

charge," Cliff said once they reached the crime scene.

The officer that stood blocking the hall looked Cliff up and down.

"It's about the murder. We may have some helpful information."

The officer hesitated before saying, "Wait right here."

He disappeared inside Felix's room, then returned, followed by a tall, thin man in a cheap-looking suit.

"I'm Detective Abraham. What can I do for you?"

Cliff indicated Ava with his thumb. "My friend was attacked yesterday by two men, and we think they may be the same men that killed Felix."

Ava stepped forward. "I'm convinced it's the same men."

"Did you file a report on the attack?"

"No, but that's not my point." She held up the handkerchief. "Whoever attacked me are the same people that killed Felix Spaulding."

"So maybe we should hire you to solve all of our crimes," the detective said sarcastically.

Ava waved the handkerchief at him. "Look, this is the handkerchief they tied my arms up with when I was attacked. My sister says it belongs to Felix Spaulding." She turned it over to where the initials were. "And it even has his initials here."

The detective reached out, took the handkerchief, and dropped it in his pocket. *Is that how they handle evidence?*

"Thank you very much. We'll make sure to look into this," he said.

"Sir," Cliff said, sensing that Ava was getting really agitated, "we are about to leave and head back to the States. If there's some information that we might be able to give you, I suggest you get it now."

The detective sighed heavily. "Did we get all of your information?"

Ava nodded.

"Well, that will be all we need." He noticed the confused looks on their faces. "Trust me, we know what we're doing, okay? Thank you for your time." He turned and walked back inside Felix's room.

Ava blew out a frustrated breath. "This is ridiculous."

Before Cliff could respond, another man stepped up to them. "Sorry to disturb you," the man said. "I'm Arthur Beckham, head of hotel security. I do understand you're leaving today, so do you mind coming down to my office so we can get an official report?"

Cliff looked to Ava, and she shrugged. "Fine, at least someone wants to talk to us."

They followed Mr. Beckham downstairs and spent thirty minutes in his office filing a report. They'd just walked out into the lobby when they heard a loud rustling noise as two police officers dragged Fredericko out of the elevator. India was hurrying right behind him.

"I want my lawyer!" Fredericko was screaming. "You can't do this. Don't you know who I am?"

Ava and Cliff watched as Fredericko struggled to break free from the handcuffs, which held his hands clamped behind his back. India looked both terrified and nervous.

"Go find me an attorney, now!" he screamed at her. "You'd better pray this all is straightened out! I'm not going to jail."

India nodded like a child who'd just been scolded, then took off back upstairs.

Ava was dumbfounded at the unfolding scene. Fredericko spotted her and jerked away from the officers holding him. "This is all your fault, you nosy bitch!"

Instinctively, Cliff stepped in front of Ava. But the cops grabbed Fredericko before he could reach her.

"I didn't kill anybody!" he screamed.

211

"And if I'd had someone killed, it would've been you!" he spat at Ava.

Ava knew she should have just kept quiet, but she found herself saying, "You did try to kill me."

Fredericko shook his head vehemently. "If I wanted my people to kill you, trust me, you'd be dead. They were just scaring you, they weren't trying . . ." His words trailed off as he realized what he was saying.

The officer who was holding his hands laughed as he hauled him toward the door. "Keep talking, big fella. You'll make our job so much easier."

Fredericko pursed his lips and shot Ava the evil eye, but didn't say another word as they dragged him to the car.

The detective they'd spoken with upstairs, Detective Abraham, walked over. "Sorry about that."

"Why didn't you tell me you were about to arrest Fredericko?" Ava asked.

Abraham smiled sourly. "I'm sorry. I didn't know that I needed to run my arrest list by you."

"No, I'm not saying that, but —"

"Look, lady, I know you watch that American news and think we're all a bunch of incompetents over here, but we do know what we're doing," Detective Abraham said.

"And we've been gathering evidence on Fredericko de la Cruz for some time now. We picked up his goons and they ratted him out."

"So they said Fredericko was behind the murder?" Cliff asked.

"No, we haven't obtained that admission yet. But they did tell us that the attack on you was ordered by Fredericko, as well as a few other unscrupulous items, enough for us to get a warrant. Trust me, I'm sure the murder will be the next charge."

Ava leaned back against the wall, a sigh of relief overtaking her.

"So it appears your drama is over. You can enjoy the rest of your vacation."

"No, this was work and I've never been more ready to go home," Ava said.

Detective Abraham laughed as he patted the paper on which he'd written her number. "I'll be in touch."

Ava looked to Cliff. "Can we please go grab my sister so we can go?"

"You took the thought right out of my head," he said, leading her to the elevator.

29

If she was supposed to be heading to the airport, why in the world was Ava standing outside India's penthouse door? *Because something isn't right.* Ava's gut told her that a piece of the puzzle was still missing. Fredericko had all but admitted he was behind the attack, yet India was still standing by him. No, something wasn't adding up and she couldn't leave Aruba until she found out what it was.

Cliff thought she was in her room packing, but she had thirty minutes, so she told herself to make one last attempt to get answers from India.

Ava pounded on the penthouse door.

"Have you lost your damn mind?" Jackie said, swinging the door open.

Ava brushed past her and stomped into the suite. "I need to see India now." Several bags were packed and set by the door, as if India, too, was about to head out.

"I'm calling security," Jackie said, racing over to the phone.

"India!" Ava called out. "I know you're hiding something, and now that my life has been endangered, I won't stop until I find out what it is!"

Jackie was grabbing Ava's arm when India emerged from a back room. Her eyes were puffy, like she'd been crying. "I don't want to hear anything you have to say."

"Just give me five minutes," Ava pleaded.

"This is ridiculous," Jackie said, walking over to pick up the phone.

"Hang up, Jackie," India said, glaring at Ava.

"I promise, I won't stay long. Just hear me out." Ava didn't know what in the world was going on. But if she was going to get any answers, India would be the one to give them to her.

India turned to Jackie. "Can you give us a moment?"

"India, are you serious?"

"Just a few minutes," India calmly said. She looked so worn-out that Ava had no doubt she was hiding something.

Jackie let out a defeated sigh as she stepped out of the room.

"I really am busy," India said. "I have to find a local attorney for Fredericko."

"That's what I'm talking about, India," Ava said. "Something isn't right. You are always in the media talking about being a strong, independent woman. All your songs are about loving yourself and being the best woman you can be, and you're letting this con man talk to you any kind of way. You're setting yourself up to allow him to take your money. I mean, you said the wedding's been called off. So why? Are you involved in his shady activities, too? That's the only reason I can think of for why you'd put up with this."

India glared at her, her eyes burning holes in Ava.

When India didn't speak, Ava continued. "I think Felix was killed because he was on to Fredericko. Something he was doing with your money."

"*My money,* exactly," India said. "So this is none of your business."

"Well, it became my business when they tried to kill me." Ava paused and studied India, who had begun nervously shaking. "Did you know about my attack? Did you order it?" she asked, the idea popping into her head.

India sighed heavily. "Of course not. I mean, I found out about the attack this morning. I had nothing to do with it." She ran her fingers through her hair as she paced before plopping down on the sofa. "I know Fredericko was behind that and it wouldn't surprise me if Fredericko had Felix killed," she said bluntly.

"What? And you're still trying to help him get an attorney?" Ava asked. She knew her instincts were right.

India sighed like she was exhausted. "I'm so tired of this," she said, leaning back on the sofa.

"Tired of what? India, what's going on?"

"Fredericko is a dangerous man," India said softly. "Felix discovered some things that really troubled him. I imagine it had to do with a lot of my money, which has come up missing, no doubt stolen by Fredericko. Felix didn't want to go into detail until he had all the facts. But if Fredericko was on to him . . ." She inhaled deeply. "Bottom line, if he killed Felix, he won't hesitate to kill anyone else who gets in the way of what he wants."

"Again, if you know that, why in the world are you helping him?"

India rolled her eyes and Ava noticed that tears had begun trickling down her cheeks. Ava softened her tone. "I'm so sorry. I know you must feel bad —"

"You can't even begin to understand what

I feel," India snapped. She closed her eyes, exhaled, then opened her eyes again. "Can we talk off the record?"

"I . . . I don't know if I'll be able to do that," Ava said. If India said something worthwhile, she wanted to be able to report it. Some journalists could care less about an off-the-record request; they'd just agree to it, and then go report it anyway. But Ava wasn't one of those people. She didn't want to commit to anything India said being off-the-record.

"Either off-the-record or you can leave right now," India said forcefully.

Ava released a defeated sigh. Curiosity had gotten the best of her, so she would hear India out — off-the-record. "Okay, we can talk off-the-record."

India still hesitated. "I know you don't know me and I don't know you, but I'm trusting that this conversation will go no farther than this room. And maybe — *woman to woman* — you will leave this alone."

"I gave my word."

India took a moment to compose herself as she dabbed at her eyes. In a weary voice she began: "I know all about Fredericko. I know everything. And I don't want to marry him, but I don't have a choice."

"I don't understand. What do you mean, you don't have a choice? Is he blackmailing you?" Ava asked.

India diverted her gaze, but the answer was evident. *"He's blackmailing you?"* Ava asked in disbelief. "But why?"

India stood, walked over to the minibar, and refilled her glass of wine. She downed half the glass before slowly turning back to face Ava. "Two years ago, there was a horrible hit-and-run accident just outside of New York," India began. "A little girl was killed. Do you remember the story?"

Ava nodded. How could she forget it? It had dominated the news for days. She, and every other journalist in town, had worked overtime on the story about the adorable little girl with blond pigtails who had been hit, her body run over so badly that her skull had been crushed. The story had outraged the community, especially because the driver had left the scene and police had never been able to find him. "I remember the story well. Her name was Kaitlyn Martin."

A pained expression crossed India's face. "Kaitlyn Martin, born June fourth, 2004. Only child of Mr. and Mrs. Donald Martin, a poor family from the Bronx who was taking Kaitlyn to her first communion. She liked bunny rabbits and had just started bal-let classes."

India seemed to be in a trance, and Ava wondered why she knew the girl's history.

"What does that little girl's death have to do with you?" Ava finally asked.

India looked miserable as she sought further reassurance. "We are talking off-the-record, right?"

Ava nodded.

"I was that hit-and-run driver."

Ava's mouth fell open.

"I was drunk," India continued in a strangled voice. "Julian and I had just left a party and I had one too many drinks. And I'm not a big drinker." She held up her glass. "Or at least I didn't used to be."

Ava was difficult to shock, but this revelation left her feeling numb all over. "If you were drunk, why would Julian let you drive?"

"He was worse off than I was. We'd all had too much to drink. We were celebrating my Grammy win."

"Why didn't you call a cab?" Ava asked.

India spoke in a low monotone. "I thought I was fine. Honestly, I don't remember much about the night, but Julian says I insisted on driving and I wouldn't wait on a car service. He said he was too out of it to fight me. Someone called Jackie to come get me since she'd left the party early. But I refused to wait."

Ava was still fighting off waves of disbelief. "Where were your bodyguards?"

"I sent them home," India said regretfully. "I was so tired of India the star. I just wanted to be India, the everyday girl who just so happened to win a Grammy. I just wanted to party with some of my friends, without all the hype."

"Well, why didn't someone else take you home?"

"I've asked myself why a thousand times. I've wished that I could go back in time, anything to make that day different. I didn't even realize what had happened until the next day when I saw my Range Rover had been damaged and a piece of her dress was caught in the mangled front grille. Jackie and Julian cleaned everything up."

"Why didn't you turn yourself in?" Ava asked more sharply. This story was almost unbelievable. And she didn't know what to think about the fact that Julian had helped her cover up a crime. Didn't that make him just as guilty?

India plopped back down on the chaise longue. "I wanted to. Believe me, I wanted to, especially after seeing the story on the news. But both Jackie and Julian convinced me that I had too much to lose. They said it would ruin me. And since Julian had helped me flee the scene, and he and Jackie had helped cover it up, they said their lives would be ruined as well."

"But you killed a little girl," Ava said, still trying to process everything.

"You think I don't know that?" India cried. Her face was full of anguish. "You think I don't live with that guilt every single day of my life? But I worked so hard to get where I am. Everyone in my family depends on me. If I fail, there are so many people that will suffer. You know my little sister has leukemia?"

Ava nodded. That had been one of the many findings in India's file.

"I have her at one of the best cancer treatment centers in the world. I'm able to pay for that because I'm this flawless *superstar*." She said *superstar* like it disgusted her. "I'm able to pay for treatment that could cure my little sister. Do you understand that? I can't do any of that behind bars. I can't do anything if my career is destroyed."

"But you killed a little girl," Ava repeated, like India was missing the point.

"I know that, which is why I wanted to turn myself in, but the more Julian convinced me, the more I started to believe it. Plus, the community was so outraged. As each day passed, I knew it would be harder to come out and confess. It soon got to the point where I felt coming forward would've only made things worse because I had waited so long."

"So you just went on about your life like everything was fine?"

India gave Ava the saddest smile she'd ever seen. "Sweetie, for me, things will never be fine again."

Ava didn't know how to respond. She could understand India's apprehension, but the fact remained — a little girl was dead because of her.

"Regardless of the hows," India continued, "Fredericko found out and is using that to blackmail me into marrying him. I even wanted to do the marriage in secret, but someone leaked it to the press, so we had to go all out and make this big production. Fredericko demanded it because *Celebrity Life* magazine offered him five hundred thousand dollars for exclusive wedding photos."

India looked at Ava with a pleading expression. "I'm telling you all of this in hopes that you'll have a heart and let this story go."

Ava momentarily wondered if India had made all of this up, but she quickly shook that thought off. No way would India lay claim to that highly publicized hit-and-run accident if it wasn't the truth.

"I'm sorry," Ava said firmly. "I understand why you wouldn't want this to get out, but I have a job to do."

"How much does that job pay you? I'll give you double your year's salary *not* to do the story." Her voice reeked of desperation.

As lucrative as the offer was, the idea of being paid off repulsed Ava. "Are you offering me a bribe?"

"Don't act like you have any ethical standards," India said, scorn filling her voice. "You work for the *National Star,* remember?"

When she said it like that, how was Ava supposed to respond? In the world of journalism, even though the *Star* paid the most money, people who worked there were at the bottom of the respectability scale. As Cliff had told her during one of their talks, you almost have to have no morals to be good at this job.

India's expression softened. "I'm sorry to snap at you like that. Yes, you can do the story and it'll make your career." Her face became bitter. "Maybe you'll get promoted.

Maybe you'll get a raise and be the darling of the magazine . . . until the next big story rolls along. Meanwhile, my life will be ruined. Julian's and Jackie's, too. My sister's health will be in jeopardy, but you'll have your story."

"Don't make this about me," Ava replied.

India looked apologetic. "Really, that's not what I'm trying to do. It's just that my going to jail will not bring that little girl back. I set up scholarships in Kaitlyn's name. I even anonymously left two hundred and fifty thousand dollars on the Martins' doorstep. Destroying me is not going to bring Kaitlyn back."

"But it's not right," Ava protested.

"Do you remember the whole nervous breakdown I had last year?"

Ava nodded. India's meltdown fifteen minutes before an appearance on *Good Morning America* had been headline news for days.

"Well, that's what caused it, the stress of trying to right my wrong. I was marrying Fredericko not just because he's blackmailing me, but as part of my punishment. So don't think I'm not paying for my crime." Her eyes filled with tears again. "You're about to destroy my life. I'm just asking you — no, I'm begging you — please don't do this. I'm not trying to buy you off, but money is all I have to offer."

"I don't want your money," Ava said, sighing heavily. "Honestly, I don't know what I'm going to do."

"Please?" India cried.

"I can't make any promises. I'm sorry." Ava headed toward the door, knowing that the devastated expression on India's face would remain etched in her mind for months to come. She'd had no idea that investigating Felix's murder would lead to the awful news of another death. All the pieces were falling into place. She had dug for the truth, and she had found it at last. Wasn't that what she was paid to do?

30

In all her years in the business, Ava had never faced a more difficult decision. Should she forget about what India had told her? Or should she pen a second article, one that would not only give Eli another blockbuster story, in turn catapulting her to fame, but also prove her investigative prowess? That would show the people over at the network what she was made of. This story could rocket her out of this tabloid life she was living and back to real reporting, but would her success rise on the ashes of India's ruin?

"No, I'm not the one who did wrong," she muttered.

"What did you say?"

Ava looked over at Cliff, who was sitting in the aisle seat. She hadn't realized she'd spoken out loud. They were on the flight heading back to New York. Mia was sitting up in first class and they were back in coach, but Ava was grateful that Cliff was sitting next to her. He'd already asked her three times what was wrong. She wanted to tell him about the bombshell India had dropped right before they left, but she held off because she wasn't sure how she was going to handle it. She felt she could trust Cliff, but at the same time she wasn't sure if she should let anyone know what she'd found out just in case she decided not to use it.

"No, sorry. Just sitting over here deep in thought."

"I see. So much so that you're holding a conversation with yourself. I must be pretty lame if you'd rather hold a conversation with yourself than me."

She flashed a warm smile at him. "You and lame? I don't think so. No, I just have a lot on my mind."

"I imagine you do after the week we've had."

Ava nodded in agreement, then peered over the rows of seats. "I'm going to run up and check on Mia."

"Okay," Cliff replied.

Ava stepped over Cliff and made her way up to first class. She was grateful to see her sister sound asleep, nestled underneath one of the thin airplane blankets. Ava didn't bother waking Mia and started back to her seat. When she passed row 11D, she saw a copy of the *National Star* lying in the empty seat next to a white-haired lady. The cover featured a gorgeous picture of India onstage at one of her concerts.

"Umm, excuse me, is this yours?" Ava asked, pointing to the magazine.

The woman looked up from her sudoku puzzle and shook her head. "Someone on the flight before us left it in the seat pocket," she said before breaking out in a mischievous grin. She leaned in and lowered her voice to a whisper. "Don't tell anyone, but I read it from cover to cover." She chuckled.

Ava managed a tolerant smile. "Do you mind if I take it?"

"Be my guest," the woman said.

Ava thanked the woman and made her way back to her seat. She immediately flipped the magazine open and began looking for her story.

"Where'd you find that?" Cliff asked when he saw the magazine.

"Some woman up toward the front." Ava stopped when she found the article. She'd seen the faxed copy India had, but this was her first time seeing it in black and white. Her heart sank as she read the story — her words, yes, but spiced up with colorful and sensational adjectives. The story made India seem like a dumb, flighty celebrity who was about to lose all of her money to an international con man. She felt sick to her stomach at the way India was portrayed.

"Hey," Cliff said, sensing her concern, "I know you feel bad, but you said yourself it was a mix-up. At the end of the day you tried to do the right thing." He reached over and gently squeezed her hand.

Ava felt comforted by his touch. *The right thing.* Yeah, she'd tried, but the bottom line remained that she hadn't done it. Ava wouldn't go so far as to say she'd ruined India's life with this article, but she'd definitely messed with her credibility and given other media outlets just cause to go digging for more.

A second article would be like throwing lighter fluid on a fire. The second article *would* ruin India's life.

At that moment, Ava decided she would wait on the second story. She was a good reporter, and a good reporter checked all her sources before starting to write. She had two sources to track down, Julian and Jackie, to confirm what India had told her.

Plus, she would have the satisfaction of seeing Julian's face when she told him what she had learned.

31

This was Ava's fifth time reading the article and the disappointment was just as strong.

Ava heard her grandmother's voice ringing in her head. *You're better than this.*

She closed her eyes and rolled her head in a circular motion on her shoulders, trying to work out the tension in her neck. With the frame of mind she was in, there was no way she'd be able to get any work done. So she gathered up her things to head out for an early lunch and maybe even pop into her massage parlor and see if they could work out the stress in her neck.

The masseuse was booked solid. Ava couldn't be sure, but she could've sworn the receptionist was looking at her with disdain, so she quickly made her exit. She'd gone to have lunch by herself, then stopped in a bookstore. That was about the only thing that could take her mind off her troubles — browsing in a bookstore. And since she was a "star" at work right now, she didn't think anything was wrong with taking a little extra time for "research." Ava found a good historical novel — her favorite — paid for it, then headed back to the office.

She had just placed the book on her desk when she looked at her keyboard to see a handwritten note, folded, with *open me* written in block letters on the front.

Ava's hand trembled as she pulled the note off her keyboard. *Ava Cole, Sept. 7, 1980–March 6, 2011.* That was tomorrow! The note was terrifying for several reasons. For starters, the person who wrote it knew her date of birth, and not only that, they'd left it sitting in the open. This meant that whoever was harassing her had access to her job.

"I am so sick of this," she mumbled as she fought back tears. Her life had been a nightmare for the three days she'd been back home. Her phone hadn't stopped ringing, despite the fact that she had an unlisted number. And now she had become the victim of the paparazzi. *Inside Edition* wanted to interview her. Even Larry King had called hoping she could give some "insight" into the bombshell story.

Ava needed a cup of coffee to calm her

nerves, so she gathered her things, told the secretary that she was leaving for the day, then left the building.

By the time Ava made it home, she was shaking uncontrollably. She felt such a sense of relief once she'd finally gotten inside her apartment. She never dreamed that her stalker would reappear in her life.

Ava had just set her purse down when her phone started ringing. She almost didn't answer it because she didn't recognize the 310 number, but since she knew that was a Los Angeles area code and she hadn't talked to Mia since they'd returned from Aruba, Ava answered.

"Hello," she said, picking up the phone before it went to voice mail.

"Hey, sissy." Mia wasn't her usual perky self, but she didn't sound as down as she had when they'd left Aruba three days ago.

"Hey, Mia. How are you doing?"

"I'm okay."

"What number is this?"

"Oh, this is my work phone, the Black-Berry Mr. Abernathy gave me. My phone is dead," Mia replied. "Anyway, sorry I haven't called. I don't really feel like talking. I mean, you know, I'm still trying to process every-thing. I didn't really know Felix all that well, but I wanted to. This whole thing creeped me out. What if I had been with him when he died? Would they have killed me, too?"

"Well, you weren't, so don't think like that," Ava said, taking a seat.

"Anyway, I'm back home and doing okay," Mia said in a lighter tone. "And I do have some good news."

"I could definitely stand to hear some good news," Ava said.

She inhaled. "Guess who called me?"

"Who?" Ava asked, not really interested in her little sister's celebrity exploits.

"Julian Lowe," she said.

"What?" Ava said, bolting upright. "For what?" Julian hadn't bothered to call and check on her, but he was calling Mia?

"Calm down," Mia said. "He wasn't calling to ask me out or anything. As a matter of fact, I went off on him for leaving you to those thugs. I think you should call him because he said there's more to that story. Anyway, he was calling because he knows I was looking for a job and he said he had someone who needed an assistant. He wouldn't tell me who it was, only that they'd won an Academy Award and I'd love working for them. Oh, my God, what if it's Tom Cruise? Or Denzel Washington?"

Ava cut into the tide of enthusiasm. "Mia, I don't have a good feeling about that."

Whatever excuse Julian came up with for leaving her, she still couldn't fathom that he'd so callously convinced India to cover up a crime.

"Of course you don't have a good feeling, because you're a worrywart," Mia said blithely. "You have enough to worry about, so don't add me to the list. I'll be fine. I'm flying in tomorrow. I'll call you then."

"Just be careful. And call me before you go off with Julian."

"Yeah, yeah, yeah," Mia said. "I'm more worried about you. Are you sure you're okay?"

"I'm fine. Just call me tomorrow, okay?"

Ava hung up and went to change into a comfortable lounging outfit. Mia's words kept ringing in her head. *You need to call him. There's more to the story.*

Ava was dropping her clothes into the hamper when she noticed Julian's business card lying on her bathroom counter. Even though she'd wondered about him, she hadn't been tempted to call, especially now that Fredericko was behind bars and her ordeal with that crew was over. But seeing the card reminded her that she still had unanswered questions. Like, did Julian know Fredericko's goons? Why would he not try to find out if she was okay? He owed her some answers.

Ava decided that the only way to get them would be to call. She picked up the card and her cell, then punched in his cell phone number.

"Hello," he said, answering on the second ring.

Ava hesitated, then said, "Hello, Julian."

He paused, like she was the last person in the world he expected to hear from. "Ava. How are you?"

She couldn't help but say, "Glad you asked. I just need to ask: Did you know Fredericko was going to have those thugs attack me?"

"Of course not," Julian said. He hesitated, then added, "I know you think I just left you, but I went for help. By the time I came back you were gone. Then" — he hesitated again — "I came by to check on you and your coworker, that Cliff guy, told me I wasn't welcome."

"What?" Cliff hadn't said anything to her about Julian coming by. In fact, he'd acted mad about Julian not bothering to check on her.

"He told me you were fine and didn't want to talk to me. So I just got on the plane and came home. India told me about Felix, and I've just kind of been in shock."

Ava couldn't believe Cliff would be so underhanded, but she wasn't going to let Julian know she was upset.

"So, did India also tell you that she filled me in on everything — you know, about the hit-and-run?" Ava said.

Silence filled the phone again.

"So, I know you were the one who convinced her to cover it up."

"I was only doing what I thought was best for my client."

"By having her cover up a crime?"

"By saving her career," he added.

"And I guess the little girl's death didn't matter to you?"

He sighed, as though he was stating the obvious. "What purpose would be served by India losing everything?"

She was so disgusted. As attracted as she was to him initially, right now he turned her stomach. All he was worried about was losing his cash cow.

"Wow," she said. "So tell me how you really feel."

He huffed, like talking to her irritated him. "Look, I gotta go. Don't run the story, all right? There's no need to ruin India's life." He hung up the phone before she could ask why he was contacting her sister.

Ava fumed at him hanging the phone up

on her, the callous way he seemed to view his cover-up, and especially the fact that he was basically blaming her for everything. Soon she found her anger drifting to Cliff. He should be at her house any moment, and she was definitely going to give him a piece of her mind.

Fifteen minutes later, she heard a knock at the front door. She opened the door to find Cliff grinning widely, Chinese food in his hands.

"I hope you're hungry," he said, holding up the containers.

"I pegged you for many things, but I never thought you to be a liar," Ava snapped.

"Excuse me?"

Ava abruptly walked back into the apartment. Cliff followed her in.

"What is your problem?" he asked.

She spun toward him. "What was the whole show, the grandstanding? 'If I see Julian, I'm going to punch him in the jaw,' " she said, mocking him. "The whole macho, testosterone thing, was it all just an act?"

"What on earth are you talking about?" Cliff said, putting the food down on the coffee table.

"I talked to Julian today."

He stared at her, looking perplexed. "And?"

"And he told me that he did come by to see me our last day in Aruba, but you ran him off. Then you want to act like he completely abandoned me."

Cliff gritted his teeth, seething. "He *did* abandon you, or do you not remember?"

"That's not the point."

"Oh, it's not? So now you're okay with him leaving you there for those thugs to do God knows what?"

"I didn't say that."

Cliff took a deep breath, trying to calm himself. "Ava, what is this really about? Are you upset that I pissed off your boyfriend?"

"For the last time, he was never my boyfriend." She folded her arms across her chest. "I just don't like liars."

He continued staring at her. She could tell her words hurt him, but if the shoe fit . . .

Suddenly, Cliff broke out in laughter. "You're a real gem, you know that?" He grabbed his keys off the table and headed for the door.

"You don't have anything to say for yourself?" she said as she followed him. "Or are you just gonna run out?"

He stopped, spun around, and glared at her. "Julian is lying! He did not come to the hotel. I did not see him. I did not say two words to him, and I don't care whether you believe me or not." He looked at her with steely eyes. "But don't worry, you've shown me what really matters."

Cliff slammed the door, and Ava was left standing in the middle of her living room, wondering what in the hell had just happened.

32

The fresh smell of lavender and roses was intoxicating. Ava leaned back in the bathtub and let the bubbles encase her. She badly needed this bath. The water was so hot it was barely tolerable. But that's what she needed to relax her nerves. Yesterday had been the day from hell with that threatening letter and the drama with Cliff. It must have really made him mad since he wouldn't answer her call last night. Then, today, as she was leaving work, Eli gave her yet another scandalous assignment. This one was about a popular politician. This came after spending all day transcribing a tape about marital problems with Kobe Bryant. She didn't even go out on the story, some other reporter did, but they had her review the tape, then write the article. That meant her name would be on the byline and yet another celebrity would be mad at her.

Ava pulled her loofah sponge out of a

nearby basket, dipped it in the bubbly water, and began gently running it over her skin as she reflected on her first few weeks on the job.

She had dreamed of being a journalist all her life. Only she had dreamed of working for prestigious papers like the *New York Times* or the *Washington Post*. Never in a million years did she think she'd end up doing celebrity gossip for a tabloid magazine.

At this thought Ava stood up in the tub and decided right then and there that she was going to stop letting this nagging voice get to her. She had a job to do and she was going to make the best of it until she could find a way to move on. She had a meeting with the network next week, and she would focus on making that the best that it could possibly be.

Ava stepped out of the tub and dried off. After rubbing her favorite lavender-rose lotion all over her body, she slipped on her silk robe. Some odd notion made her look outside her living room window. Ever since she'd received that note, she kept worrying that her stalker was loitering outside her building, just waiting for the right time to strike.

That's why she nearly jumped when the

doorbell rang in the front hall. All the way down the stairs, she checked to see if she recognized the silhouette of the person standing on her stoop. As she came close, she realized that she did. It was Cliff.

"Ava, it's Cliff, open up!"

Ava shook herself out of her daze and raced to let him in. She was so grateful to see him.

"Hey, Ava. I came to apologize. Can I come in?" he gently asked when Ava didn't respond. Worry lines creased his face.

Ava took one look at him, then sank into his arms. She needed somebody to hold her so bad. Cliff hugged her and stroked her hair while she inhaled and welcomed his touch.

"I'm so sorry," she told him. "I'm sorry I doubted you. I should've at least asked you before just jumping on you. It's just that —"

"Shhh," Cliff said, putting a finger to her lips. "Don't worry about it."

She was grateful for his forgiveness. "When you rang the doorbell, I thought you were the stalker." She laughed at her paranoia. "Like a stalker would ring the doorbell."

Cliff was instantly alarmed. "What? Is he back?"

Ava picked up the latest note from the front hall table, and she showed it to him.

"Don't worry," he said firmly after reading the note. "I'm here to protect you."

Ava's first instinct was to say she didn't need protection. But she did. In fact, she welcomed it.

Cliff softly stroked her face. "Are you sure you're okay?"

Ava nodded as she felt herself tear up. "I am, especially now that you're here."

"Well, even though you treat me like dirt," he said with a smile, "I consider you my friend, and I would be less than a friend if I let you deal with this on your own."

Ava laid her head on Cliff's shoulder. Having Cliff here with her, she'd never felt more safe.

Cliff stayed with her until late that evening. When it was time for him to leave, she wanted desperately to ask him to stay. Instead she walked him down the stairs.

"Thanks for coming back," Ava said.

He looked at her longingly. "Anytime." Cliff hesitated, then before she could say anything, he leaned in and kissed her passionately. It was the most intense kiss she'd ever experienced. She pulled away, slightly dazed.

"I would apologize," he said, "but I'm not

sorry. I don't care about your rule about work and play. I am so attracted to you."

She smiled bashfully. "The feeling's mutual." She tilted up her head. "So, why don't we try that one more time?"

33

The buzz of her BlackBerry woke Ava. She hadn't even realized that she'd dozed off.

Ava fumbled around until she grabbed the phone. She pulled herself up and looked groggily at the screen. Yet when she read the text, she bolted upright.

Hey, sis. In town. Meeting w/Julian @ Casimir. Battery low but will call u later.

Ava immediately punched in her sister's number anyway. Her heart sank when it went directly to voice mail.

She stood up and began pacing. This wasn't making sense. Why was Julian really contacting Mia? She grabbed his business card and punched in his number as well. His phone also went to voice mail.

Ava knew she'd go out of her mind sitting there wondering what Julian was up to. She didn't have a choice. She had to go see for herself.

She caught a cab and in thirty minutes

was standing in front of the crowded bistro on Avenue B. Ava stood by the door and scanned the restaurant until she saw Julian and Mia at a back table. She had the impulse to walk over when a woman in a big-brimmed hat and large shades nearly knocked her over. The woman didn't bother apologizing. Ava was about to say something when she recognized the woman. *What is Jackie doing here?*

Jackie was a woman on a mission. She stopped when she spotted Julian and Mia, then instead of walking over to the table, she pulled out her cell phone. Ava watched the exchange, her face averted. Julian's phone rang, and he pulled it out. He must have pressed Ignore because he dropped it back into his pocket.

Jackie was fuming as she punched the numbers into her phone again. This time Julian answered.

"What the hell are you doing?" Jackie hissed. Julian kept a smile on his face as he replied. "I don't think so," Jackie continued. "I'm not going anywhere. . . . Meet me in the ladies room in one minute. . . . I'm not playing with you, Julian. . . . Either you come now or . . ."

Ava didn't stick around to hear her finish her sentence. Instead she darted toward the ladies room at the end of the front hallway. Spotting four stalls inside, she ducked in the last one. She quickly stood on the toilet and left the door cracked open to make it look like no one was in the stall.

A few seconds later, Ava heard the angry click of stilettos enter the restroom. Instinct told her to ease her digital recorder out of her purse, which she did and softly pressed Record.

The door opened again, and Ava heard what sounded like the click of a lock, then Julian's voice.

"Is anyone in here?"

"What does it look like?" Jackie responded.

"What the hell are you doing here?"

"No, the real question is, what are you doing here with her?"

"Look, I'm trying to work this out. This girl may be the ticket to make that happen. I need to find out how much Ava knows." His voice dropped, becoming more of a growl. "I cannot have you following me around. You're going to mess everything up. I don't need Mia getting suspicious. I got rid of her now, but she's not as dumb as she looks."

Jackie huffed and continued talking. "Everything is falling apart. You told me that by now we'd be relaxing on a tropical island somewhere."

"Well, it's taken a little longer for things to fall apart with India," Julian replied. He sounded stressed.

Jackie started pacing, her stilettos clicking. "I'm tired of this, Julian. You have strung me along for too long. I covered for you when you had that damn accident and killed the little girl. I went along with this cockamamy plan to blame India because you told me to look at the bigger picture. Well, I'm still looking and the picture has not started to emerge."

"Calm down. We had been looking for a way to get out from under India, and that accident was our ticket out."

"Obviously, it wasn't," Jackie said. "Her life hasn't been ruined and we're still waiting!"

Ava's mouth dropped open in disbelief as she listened.

"I expected her to have a complete breakdown after the accident. I can't help it if she pulled herself together," Julian said.

"You should've let her confess."

"No, because then that would've ruined everything. She hadn't signed over the power of attorney yet. I hadn't gotten everything situated."

"Is it situated now?"

"I'm working on it. I have a plan."

"We've seen how well your plans work."

"Just listen. With Felix out of the picture, it's just a matter of time before she brings someone else in. So I'm going to find a way to make her give us enough money to get out of town."

"*That's* your brilliant plan? Just get India to give us some money?"

"Do you have a better suggestion?"

Jackie groaned in exasperation.

"It's just a matter of time before those Keystone Kops in Aruba put two and two together and figure out Fredericko had nothing to do with Felix's murder."

"I don't understand why you had to kill him."

"Because he was getting too close. What do you think he was meeting with India about? He'd found out about the missing money. The damn accountant turned out to be a computer whiz, because he broke into files that were supposed to be locked." Julian sighed. "I just need you to trust me, baby."

"Trust you? Aren't you the same person who got drunk around that asshole Fredericko and told him the whole freaking story? And what does he do with that informa-

250

tion? Blackmails you and India!"

"I thought he was my friend. I didn't expect him to use it against me."

"You didn't expect a lot of things, it seems." Her voice was full of frustration. "You said you were going to work that reporter over, make sure she did the damaging story. Only you pick a tabloid reporter with a conscience."

"It's not like I had any control over who the *National Star* sent. Don't you see? The fact that they sent some lonely woman that I could easily work over, all of that was divine intervention. I know it looked like things were going off course, but I handled that, babe."

Ava had to steady herself. All this time she thought Fredericko was behind everything and it was Julian?

"Don't think I've forgotten about you being all up in that tramp's hotel room," Jackie said.

"Look, can you stay focused on the bigger picture? I told you nothing happened. Besides, I'm glad I was in her room or else I wouldn't have been able to send both stories."

Ava listened in disbelief. She wouldn't have believed it if she hadn't heard it with her own two ears. He was the one who sent

the story to Eli? That bastard had been using her.

"Look," Julian continued, "I'm just as sick
and tired of the whole charade as you. I
don't —"

Without warning Ava's foot slipped, and
she squealed as she grabbed the stall parti-
tion to keep from falling. She silently cursed
as Julian and Jackie got quiet. She heard
their footsteps heading toward her stall.
Think, Ava, she told herself. She knew it was
just a matter of seconds before they opened
the stall and saw her, so she did the only
thing she knew how. She slammed the door
open, knocking Jackie to the ground as she
jumped off the toilet and raced out the door
like her life depended on it.

"Hey," she heard Julian's furious voice call
after her, "come back here!"

34

Ava was a nervous wreck as she fled the restaurant. She had immediately called Cliff and headed to his place. She didn't want Julian trying to find out where she lived and come track her down. Of course, Cliff had been speechless as she recounted the details of Jackie and Julian's conversation.

"Have you talked to Mia?"

"She's still not answering her phone. Where did she go?" Ava rubbed her temple. "Hopefully, she'll call soon."

"So what's next?" Cliff asked.

Ava paced across the room. "I have no idea. I could always go to the police. I do have the tape."

"Yeah, I definitely think that's a good idea, but in the meantime, he's still going to try to come after you."

Ava felt tears welling up. How had her life turned into this? From the threatening letters — she still didn't know where those

253

were coming from — to Fredericko having her attacked in Aruba to now Julian trying to hunt her down, Ava couldn't help but wonder if her investigative reporting would catch up to her.

"Okay, we could go to the cops. But the tape is all we have. I don't think that's even going to be admissible in court because I illegally taped it. The last thing I need is for something to get thrown out on a technicality, and I spend the rest of my life in fear." Ava continued her pacing. "And I need to at least tell India. She's been carrying around this guilt over the accident, and she didn't even cause it."

Cliff took her in his arms and hugged her tightly. "I'm sorry you're stressed. But you're right. You need to at least talk to India. Then you guys can take it from there."

Ava pulled back. "I don't even know how to get in touch with her."

"You're an award-winning investigative journalist. If anyone can find India Wright, you can."

It was refreshing to hear those words, although Ava didn't know if she believed then. Even still, she said, "Let's get to work."

It took all night and nearly an act of Congress to find India. Even though Ava still hadn't talked to Mia, she had sent a text saying Mr. Abernathy had summoned her back to L.A. for business. That helped Ava relax and she was able to focus and put her investigative skills to work to track down India's attorney, Marco DeLeon. He initially gave Ava the cold shoulder, but when she told him about the tape, he'd agreed to give her five minutes.

Now those five minutes had turned to forty-five, and by the time they were done, he too was dumbfounded.

"That low-down snake," Marco muttered.

"Tell me about it," Ava said. "He used me and I'm pissed. I can only imagine how India is going to feel."

"So do you think this is enough?" Cliff asked. They were sitting in Marco's lavish Manhattan office.

"I don't know, but we're sure about to see." Marco gathered up his things. "I have a friend in the district attorney's office. I'll check with him. I agree that the tape won't be admissible because you were illegally recording, but if we can get Jackie to crack, that's all we'll need. Let me call India. If I can get her to agree to it, I'd like for you to deliver this news personally," he told Ava.

Ava nodded. "Of course."

"Well, I'll get back with you two later."

Ava and Cliff followed him out of his office. She let out a sigh of relief once they were outside. Was India's nightmare about to end? She sure hoped so because then maybe hers would, too.

"Do you want to go get something to eat?" Ava asked as they headed toward the subway station. "Maybe we can kill some time until Mr. DeLeon catches up with India."

Over lunch they talked about everything but work. He was trying, and succeeding, to get her mind off the drama that had become her life. She learned he was from a small town in Alabama, so he could relate to her desire to stay in the big city. Both of them had gone to college on scholarships. He was from a big family but only wanted one or two children himself. They had similar tastes in everything from sports to movies to recreational activities. It's almost like everything about him was what Ava had been seeking in a man. What struck her most about Cliff was his overwhelming desire to settle down.

"I guess you can call me old school," he said. "I don't want to have a kid out of wedlock. I grew up in a two-parent household, and that's what I want for my kid."

She admired that about him. His commitment to always do the right thing was certainly appealing.

"So, be honest, there's no one you're see-ing?" Ava asked.

"I told you, I have lots of friends," he said with a smile. "No, for real, I date, but they're nothing serious. They're not mar-riage material. They're kind of like Sally, the girl from Aruba. They just want to have a good time."

At the mention of Sally's name, Ava felt a twinge of jealousy again. She was just about to say something else when her phone rang.

"Excuse me," she said, picking it up. She didn't recognize the number, but answered just in case it was India's attorney.

"Hello, Miss Cole." It was Marco. Ava felt her heartrate speed up.

"Hi, Mr. DeLeon."

He didn't waste any time. "She'll talk to you," he said. "It wasn't easy, but she's wait-ing on you now. Hope you can get over there."

"Not a problem. I can go right now." She gave Cliff a thumbs-up. He mouthed, *Great.*

"I would meet you there, but I'm still in court," DeLeon continued. "Besides, I really think you need to be the one to deliver this news."

"I know, because she hates me," Ava said.

"You said it, not me." He laughed. "I'm giving you her address. I'm trusting you with this, Miss Cole," he said firmly. "No one is to know where she lives."

"Believe it or not, I'm really not a scum-bag reporter. I assure you that I will not give this information to anyone."

"Okay," he said. "She's waiting on you."

"I'm on my way."

Cliff had already pulled out the money to pay for their meal and was pushing back from the table by the time Ava hung up the phone.

"Great, let's get over there. We'll tell her everything, they'll lock up Julian and Jackie, and you can feel better about this mess."

Ava breathed a sigh of relief. She could only hope it would be that easy.

35

If looks could kill, Ava would definitely be six feet under. India stood in the doorway and glared at her, utter disdain blanketing her face. Ava was struck by how bad she looked. Her hair was pulled back into a rough ponytail. She wore a frumpy gray sweat suit and no makeup. Her eyes were puffy and red. A far cry from the diva Ava had first met in Aruba.

Her home, on the other hand, was fit for a star. Her twenty-eighth floor condo commanded a dramatic view of the city. The entire apartment was decked out with contemporary white leather furniture. And each wall was covered with exquisite art, with the exception of the wall that housed her numerous awards.

"Thank you for making time to talk with me," Ava said.

India grunted noncomittally. "When Marco called and said you wanted to talk, I told him you must want more dirt." She folded her arms across her chest. "He assured me that I needed to hear you out."

Ava understood India's nervousness. Once she had confessed about the hit-and-run, she must have suffered agony, wondering when doom would finally strike.

"I came here to tell you about a plot to steal your money," Ava said.

"Is that so?"

"Yes, it is. And it involves both Julian and Jackie. They're behind everything."

India turned up her lips in disbelief. "Let me get this straight. You expect me to believe Julian, my manager and my friend for the last fifteen years, and Jackie, my friend for life, conspired against me?"

"Yes, Julian and Jackie. They were working together."

"I know you're talking crazy. I'll repeat: Jackie has been my best friend since elementary school."

"Don't take my word for it." Ava pulled out the tape recorder and pressed Play. She had it cued up and ready to go because she knew India wouldn't believe her. The sounds of Julian's and Jackie's voices filled the air. India listened in growing horror. By the time the recording had stopped, India had not only a look of disbelief on her face, but tears had started filling her eyes.

"Is . . . is this some kind of joke?" she asked.

"I wouldn't play around with something like this," Ava replied.

"But . . . Julian . . . and Jackie . . . how could they?" India stammered.

"I'm sorry to be the bearer of bad news," Ava said. "But do you know what this means?"

India fell against the wall, almost knocking over a vase that looked like it cost as much as Ava made in a month. "It means the two people I trusted most in this world betrayed me," she said as her brow furrowed like she was trying to make sense of everything.

Ava eased over and gently put a hand on India's arm. "No. It means you didn't cause the accident. The hit-and-run accident that killed little Kaitlyn Martin was not your fault."

India's hand went to her mouth. "Oh, my God," she said as if that had just dawned on her. "I was set up."

"Yes. And you've been punishing yourself for something you didn't do."

India had to take a seat. She looked weak as she held the wall and walked over to a leather high-back chair.

"Can I get you something?" Ava asked.

India dabbed her eyes. "I'm fine." Her forehead filled with lines of intense concentration. "There are so many times that something didn't feel right with Jackie," she said quietly. "And I just blew it off because I knew she was bitter."

"About what?"

India took a deep breath to compose herself. "Jackie and I started a singing group when we were in high school. We got a small record deal. It flopped, but afterward the producer signed me to a solo deal. They had no interest in Jackie. I wasn't going to take the offer, but Jackie said she was okay with it. She told me at least one of us could be a star. I guess she's never gotten over that." India shook her head. "I just never thought it would drive her to this. Conspiring with Julian? This is just unbelievable."

"What are you going to do?"

India shook her head, as though shaking off her disbelief. "Let me make a call." She grabbed her cell phone off the coffee table. India punched in a number, then quickly rattled off what she'd just learned. "That's what I thought," she said after a few minutes of back-and-forth conversation. "Okay, I'll be in touch." She hung up the phone and turned back to Ava. "That was Marco. He double-checked. The tape definitely won't hold up in court. The police can't even use it to bring them in for questioning. I mean, I now know I'm not responsible for the hit-and-run, but I have no way of proving it."

"So what do we do?" Ava asked.

"Marco said we have to get Jackie to admit everything and testify against Julian."

"How are you going to do that?"

India thought about it for a few moments. Finally, she said, "Jackie is terrified of prison. All I have to do is make her believe that she can spend a long time behind bars, and she'll tell us everything we need to know. She'll turn on Julian in a heartbeat. And I have just the plan to make her do it."

Ava nodded and listened intently as India laid out her plan. She hoped it would work because the last thing she wanted was for Julian and Jackie to get away with what they'd done — to India and to her.

36

"So, do you really think India's plan will work?" Cliff asked.

They were snuggled up on his sofa. He'd tried to get Ava to watch a movie and relax. She'd been a nervous wreck not only because of everything that was going on but because she still hadn't talked to her sister. She needed to let Mia know everything that was going on so she would know to stay far away from Julian.

The only saving grace was knowing that her sister had left town.

"Ava, did you hear me? I said, do you think the plan will work?"

Ava shook herself out of her thoughts. "I'm sorry. My mind is racing a million miles a minute."

"Understandably so." He stood. "You know what, I'm going to pour you a glass of wine to help you relax."

"Thanks." Ava managed a smile as she

watched him walk off.

He looked back and caught her staring at him. "Don't be looking at my butt. I feel so violated," he joked, covering his behind.

She appreciated his attempts to lighten the situation.

Cliff returned and handed her a glass of wine. "I meant to ask you, have you had any more letters?"

Ava shook her head as she took the drink. "No, thank goodness. Maybe someone was upset over a story I did, although these letters really freaked me out."

"Well, I had planned on sticking around to protect you. So you let me know if you get any more."

She smiled. "Yes, sir." This time she didn't feel like he was interfering. She loved knowing that someone was ready to have her back.

Cliff returned to his seat next to her on the sofa. "So, you and India are going to try to do this tomorrow?"

Ava nodded. "We are. I go over there in the morning. You know, India found out they've stolen almost five hundred grand from her over the last three years."

"Wow," Cliff said. "How do you have that much money stolen and not miss it?"

"Because she trusted both of them and

she admits she rarely checked on them. That's what she believes Felix discovered."

He took Ava's feet and propped them up on his lap. "Do you think Jackie knows that India is on to them?"

"India said she was going to call Jackie and act like everything was fine. Maybe Jackie and Julian will just think I skipped town. So she shouldn't see anything coming."

Worry lines creased his face. "I still don't know about this."

"She's not dangerous, Cliff. Julian may be, but she's not." Just thinking of Julian sent her blood boiling again. In Aruba she had felt rejuvenated, sexy with him. Now images of the two of them made her skin crawl. "What's even more disgusting about this," Ava added, "is that both Julian and Jackie knew how much the thought of killing that little girl was tearing India apart and they let her think she did it anyway."

"Did he really think she'd sign over all her money?" Cliff asked.

"Yeah, and I wouldn't have been surprised if she had. She had complete trust in him and Jackie."

Cliff shook his head. "See, that's exactly why you have to be careful who you trust."

"Do I have to be careful with you?" Ava

asked, her voice turning serious. She was tired of talking about Julian and Jackie, and even India. They'd consumed her life since she'd left for Aruba. She wanted to focus on her own life, her own happiness. She'd wasted years waiting on Phillip to come around. She was ready to start living, and the more time she spent with Cliff, the more she knew she wanted Cliff to be a part of that life.

"No, the question is, do I have to be careful with *you?*" he replied, just as serious.

She sat up. "What does that mean?"

He shrugged like he didn't really want to get into it. "Never mind."

"No, Cliff, tell me what's on your mind."

He looked at her pensively, then lovingly brushed hair out of her face. "I just want to make sure you're not hanging out with me on the rebound."

"What do you mean?"

"I mean, you just broke up with your fiancé."

"Yeah, but if I'm honest with myself, I know we've been over for a long while."

"And just last week you were lusting after another man."

"I was lonely and vulnerable," she said. "I'm not saying I want to marry you tomorrow, but I am saying I don't have to wait six months to know I want to see where things with you can go."

He nodded thoughtfully. "Okay, I'll take that. One more question."

"Yes?"

"What was it about Julian? You know, I was interested in you from the moment I saw you, but you only had eyes for him."

"Oh, believe me, I thought you were attractive from day one, but I didn't want to mix business with pleasure." She didn't bother mentioning the whole sex-appeal thing. She'd deduced that was what was wrong with so many relationships — people were worried about sex appeal. She just wanted someone who could bring her joy.

"So you changed your mind?" Cliff asked.

"I'll take my pleasure where I find it."

He smiled. "That's music to my ears."

"But let me be clear. I want to be your friend."

That wiped the smile off his face.

"My friend?"

"*And* your lover," she quickly added.

He licked his lips and nodded in satisfaction. "Last question." He held up one finger. "Am I your only friend-slash-lover?"

"The only one I want," she replied. "If you'll have me."

He grinned widely. "Then it's official.

You're all mine." He leaned in and kissed her. It wasn't a passionate kiss that sent fireworks through her body. But it was slow and deliberate. It sent a different kind of feeling through her. One of joy, happiness, and anticipation of where this relationship was headed.

37

When Ava's doorbell rang, she assumed Cliff had come back for something. He'd left about ten minutes ago. Ava was surprised to see Phillip at her front door. They hadn't talked since he walked out on her a few weeks ago. She realized that she hadn't even thought about him since she'd returned from Aruba.

"Hi, Phillip," she said.

He stared at her uneasily, like he didn't know how to gauge her pleasant demeanor. "Hey. How are you?"

"I'm fine."

"Well, I um, I have a few more things that I need to pick up. A couple of things in the upstairs guest room."

"Oh, I forgot about that stuff in the closet up there." She stepped aside. "Well, come on in."

He eased by her, still eyeing her suspiciously. "Sorry I didn't call, but I was —"

"Don't worry about it," she said flatly. "Get what you need."

"Are you okay?"

She shut the door. "Yes, I'm fine. Why?"

"Well, you know, our breakup and everything."

Nice of you to call and check before now, she wanted to say, but she didn't bother. Instead she said, "Thank you for your concern, but I'm doing fine." She frowned at the way he was studying her. "Why do you have that look on your face?"

He shrugged. "I don't know. It's just that you're being rather, um, I guess the word I'm looking for is *nice.*"

She chuckled. "What do you want me to do, Phillip? Cry, curse, scream?"

"I know we didn't end on the best of terms."

"No, we didn't, but truthfully, you were right. We were finished long before the day you walked out."

He fumbled with the edge of his jacket. "Well, I just want you to know that at one time I truly did love you."

"Thank you for telling me that." She really had no desire to hear anything he had to say. She wanted him to grab his junk and leave.

He continued. "But the more time wore

on, the more I saw that I just wanted a traditional wife and you're far from traditional."

"That I am," she said matter-of-factly.

"I hope there are no hard feelings."

"There aren't." Part of her wanted to rub her budding relationship in his face. But she decided against it. "You can go ahead and get your stuff." She pointed to the stairs. "I'm in here doing some work."

"Okay, I won't be long."

"Take your time."

Ava returned to the sofa and opened her laptop. Phillip had been upstairs about ten minutes when she heard a banging at her front door.

"What in the world?" Ava mumbled as she entered the hallway.

The person was banging like there was a fire somewhere. Ava glanced out the peephole. A woman with long, disheveled brown hair was beating on the door like a madwoman.

"May I help you?" Ava said through the door.

"Where's Phillip?" the woman screamed. "I know he's in there. I followed him here!"

"You'd better get away from my door before I call the police," Ava warned.

"Open this door!" the woman screamed back.

Ava grabbed the baseball bat she kept next to her door. "Are you crazy?" Ava said, opening the door.

The woman didn't respond as she barged past Ava into the foyer.

"Phillip! Phillip, get your ass down here!"

Ava frowned. "Who are you and why are you in my house screaming like you've lost your mind?"

"Because I have." She spun toward Ava. "I'm so sick and tired of you. Why can't you go away?"

Ava's right eyebrow shot up. "Excuse me?"

"Phillip is mine," the woman spat. "He's been mine. And he would've been mine sooner if he didn't feel sorry for you."

"Sorry for me for what?"

The woman put her hands on her hips and tilted her head. "Because you're dying and he didn't want to hurt you."

The unexpected excuse made Ava break out in laughter. "I'm sorry. I don't know what my ex-fiancé told you, but I assure you, I have a clean bill of health."

Before the woman could respond, Phillip appeared at the top of the stairs. "Sharla?"

The woman spun toward him, her eyes blazing.

"What are you doing here?" Phillip said, making his way down the steps.

She folded her arms across her chest. "No, the question is, what are *you* doing here? You said you were going to see one of your friends."

"That's because I didn't want to hear your mouth," he growled.

"Why are you here with *her?*" Sharla cried.

"I came to pick up some stuff," he said through gritted teeth. "Why are you following me?"

"Because I could tell you were lying. And I just knew you were coming" — she turned and jabbed a finger toward Ava — "to this tramp's house."

"Wow," Ava said in amazement. "Is this really happening?"

Sharla stepped in Ava's face. "I'm Phillip's girlfriend. He lives with me now, so you need to stay the hell away from him."

"Look, Phillip," Ava interjected, glaring at Sharla. "You and your girlfriend, or whoever the hell she is, need to take your drama and get out of my place."

"You need to get out of our lives and move on. Accept it, it's over." What Ava had said earlier must have finally registered because she spun back toward Phillip. "She said

274

she's not sick. Were you lying to me?"

Phillip sighed in exasperation but didn't answer her.

"You said the only reason you were staying with her was because she was dying."

Ava finally spoke up. This was getting ridiculous. "I don't know what he told you, or how long the two of you have been together. Frankly, I don't care," Ava said, her anger starting to boil. "But I can tell you this," she added, glaring at Phillip. "I'm not sick or dying, and Phillip has been free to leave at any time. He knows that all he had to do was say he wanted out and I would've helped him pack."

Tears began welling up in Sharla's eyes as she stared at Phillip. "So why did you lie?"

Phillip stared blankly at her.

"All this time, for over a year, you've been stringing me along, telling me this lie about her dying, what was that about?" Sharla cried. "Everything I did to get us to be together. I changed my hair because you told me to. I stopped sending the letters because you said it would stress her out and you wanted her to die peacefully, and it was all a lie?"

Ava's mouth dropped open. "*You* were the one sending me letters?"

"You were standing in the way of my

dreams," she declared with no shame. "You were the reason I wasn't having my happily ever after."

"Unbelievable" was all Ava could say. And to think she thought the notes were penned by someone she'd done a story on, and all along it was her fiancé's mistress? Oh, this was too much. Ava turned to Phillip. "You knew I was getting these letters, how much they were freaking me out. If I recall, you said, maybe if I stopped pissing people off, the harassment would end. But all along, you knew the woman you were cheating with was sending me the letters?"

Phillip was totally busted. "Ava, it's not like that at all."

"You know what, Phillip?" Ava raised the bat and pointed it at him. "I need you and your tramp to get out of my house."

"I'm a tramp that is about to marry your man, something you couldn't get him to do."

"You say that like it's a good thing," Ava said.

"All I know is you'd better stay away from Phillip."

Ava swung the bat and knocked over a lamp, causing everyone to jump as it shattered in a hundred little pieces. "One more time! Get the hell out of my house!" She shook the bat at Sharla. "Because the next thing this bat makes contact with will be your head."

Phillip grabbed his box. "Let's go," he said as he stomped toward the door. Sharla scuttled out after him.

"Phillip, I'm sorry for following you. I'm just so scared of losing you. Please forgive me," she whined as she followed him.

"Just shut up," he said as he flung the door open.

Ava was dumbfounded. Sharla just found out her boyfriend had lied to her and she was the one begging for forgiveness? That was absolutely insane. Ava closed and locked her door, making a mental note to get her locks changed.

She released a long sigh. What a day. Yet despite the drama, she felt a sense of relief knowing who was behind those letters. And if that crazy woman was Phillip's idea of a "traditional" wife, then she was glad they hadn't gotten married after all.

38

Ava felt like an undercover agent. She waved to the security guard, who had been instructed to allow her and Cliff in.

"Are you sure you don't want me to go in with you?" Cliff asked once they'd reached the elevator.

"I'm positive. You can't come in or it might blow everything."

"Well, I'll be right here," Cliff said. "You just call me. I am on your speed dial, right?"

"Number one," she said, smiling, holding up the phone. They stepped onto the elevator. "But calm down. I told you I don't think Jackie is dangerous. Bitter maybe. But not lethal."

"I don't want to take any chances. Are you sure you don't want this?" He patted his jacket pocket.

Ava bucked her eyes as she looked around nervously. "You brought that? I told you I wasn't fooling with any guns!"

Cliff looked uncomfortable. "Look, I just got you. I'm not about to lose you." Impulsively, he pulled her close, and his gesture warmed her heart.

"You won't lose me." She kissed him — and this time she did feel sparks shoot through her body. "Now, keep that tucked away," she said, patting his pocket as the elevator door opened. They stepped off. "I'm sure we won't need it."

"Well, just so you know, I'll be right outside the door. If I hear anything out of the ordinary, I'm busting in."

"Okay, Billy the Kid. We'll be fine. Just wait over there." She pointed to the end of the hallway. "I can do this."

He still looked unsure, but he leaned in and kissed her on the lips. "Be careful."

"I will. Now go." She swatted him away and he darted down the hall, ducking behind the wall.

Ava took a deep breath, then rang India's doorbell.

A long moment passed, then Jackie flung the door open. "May I help you?" Panic was written all over her face.

"I need to see India."

She took a defensive stance. "Well, India doesn't want to see you!"

"I just need a minute."

"What do you want? Haven't you done enough damage?"

Ava put on her best sympathetic face. "I just wanted to tell her I'm sorry again and let her know I'm doing a follow-up interview."

"Are you serious?" Jackie said. "Do you think she wants to talk to you?"

Ava smiled knowingly. "I'm sure she does."

"Was that you the other day?" Jackie whispered in a panic.

"Let her in."

Jackie's face winced in alarm, and she looked back over her shoulder. "India, you don't need to talk to her. Why would you even give her the time of day?"

"I want to hear about this follow-up story," India said.

"Don't trust her. You saw what happened the last time you trusted her!"

"Just let her in," India said.

Jackie's eyes spit fire as Ava stepped past her.

"What do you want?" India said, feigning anger.

"Julian, your manager, has me feeling bad, and he said you might be open to talking to me and doing another story."

"What does Julian have to do with anything?" India asked.

"India, you need to put her out. She's a freaking gossip reporter." Jackie tried to grab Ava's arm, but Ava jerked it free.

India turned her nose up. "Jackie, what's wrong with you? Calm down."

"I just don't think you should waste time talking to her. She's just going to screw you over," Jackie repeated.

"Yeah," India said, no longer able to contain her anger. "Kinda like you're screwing me."

Jackie looked confused. "Excuse me?"

India advanced until she was nose to nose with Jackie. "How could you do this to me?" she said through gritted teeth.

"What are you talking about?"

"I know all about you and Julian," India spat.

She took a step back. "What? What's going on?" she said, looking back and forth between India and Ava.

"Should we play the tape?" India asked, not taking her eyes off Jackie.

"I think we should." Ava reached into her bag, pulled out the recorder, and pressed Play. Jackie's voice filled the room. Her eyes bucked in horror as she listened to the tape.

"Oh, are we speechless now?" India asked after the tape stopped playing. She glared at

Jackie. "How could you do this to me?"

"I . . . I can explain," Jackie stammered.

"Can you? Really? You can explain the fact that Julian killed a little girl, then blamed me, and you went along with it? The two of you were behind Felix's murder because he caught on to the fact that you were stealing my money. Are you serious? You low-down, conniving bitch!"

Jackie's cowed expression suddenly changed. "Oh, don't get all holier than thou on me," she hissed. "You were as drunk as all get out at that party. It could've just as easily been you behind the wheel as Julian."

"But it wasn't," India fired back. "You knew the guilt I was feeling. You knew the pain I endured. Hell, you even held me as I cried night after night, and it was all a lie!" India looked at Jackie as though she were seeing a new type of creature. "I thought you were my friend."

"Friend?" Jackie barked a maniacal, intense laugh. "Are you for real? *Friends?* Friends don't just toss each other to the wind when a good deal comes along. We were in this thing together, and you threw me aside the first chance you got!"

"So that's what this is about? Because I was offered a solo record deal ten years ago and I took it?"

"No, because I'm a better singer," she said with conviction. "I work harder, I sound better, but you bat your pretty little eyes and flash that big ol' behind of yours and now suddenly you're the one with star material!"

"Yes, you're a better singer. I'll give you that," India replied evenly. "But you have a funky attitude and nobody wants to deal with you. And the bottom line is that while you may sing better, you're not a better performer, and in this business, that matters just as much as talent." India let out a dejected sigh. "I never in a million years would've thought that you would be capable of something like this."

Jackie rolled her eyes. "Oh, boo-hoo-hoo."

"Did it mean that much to you that you would stab me in the back to steal my money?" India continued.

"We didn't try. We did," she said, her voice full of arrogance. "You're so busy being cute, filming your movies, and dating your celebrities that you didn't even realize we were living high off your money."

India looked at her in pity. "I would've given you anything you asked for," she said softly. "I mean, I already paid both of you six-figure salaries."

"I'm a damn assistant!" Jackie screamed.

"A freaking glorified gopher!"

"You know you were so much more than that."

Jackie threw up her hands. "Whatever, India. Do you think I want to be your errand girl for the rest of my life? I have dreams, too. Dreams you destroyed because, as always, you have to come out on top. It's been that way since middle school!"

Her arrogance was amazing. Even so, while Ava wasn't an expert on crime-scene techniques, she didn't think what Jackie had just said constituted a confession. She knew that she had to step in.

Ava didn't know where she was going, but she knew she had to get Jackie even more worked up. She had to turn Jackie against Julian so she'd be willing to testify against him.

"I'm shocked at all of this," Ava said. "When Julian and I slept together in Aruba, he acted like he couldn't stand you."

Jackie shot an evil eye at Ava. "You lying whore. Julian didn't sleep with you."

"Ummm, I know that's what he told you," Ava coolly replied. "But you don't really think he was in my hotel room and nothing happened, huh?" She made a sisterly gesture, holding out her head. "Don't worry, I feel used, too. Sexually satisfied, but used nonethe—"

Jackie lunged at Ava before she could finish her sentence. They'd anticipated that, and Michael, India's bodyguard, bolted out of the hallway and grabbed Jackie from behind just before her long fingernails made contact with Ava.

Jackie kicked and screamed, but when she saw Michael wasn't releasing his firm grip, she took a deep breath. "Let me go," she panted.

"Not until you calm down," Michael said, shaking her.

"Let her go," India said sadly.

Jackie snatched her arms away as Michael released her. She and India stood like they were in a face-off. Tears filled India's eyes. She didn't say a word for a minute, then simply glanced toward the corner of the room. "You guys can come out now."

A flash of panic came over Jackie's face. Ava stood back as the side doors opened and four men in gray suits entered the room.

"What is this?" Jackie said, her eyes darting from one to the other.

One of the men walked in front of Jackie. "Jackie Baptiste, you are under arrest for grand larceny and obstruction of justice."

"What? I didn't do anything," Jackie cried.

"You have the right to remain silent.

Anything you say can and will be used against you in a court of law. You have the right to an attorney. If you cannot afford an attorney, one will be appointed to you. Do you understand these rights as they have been read to you?" the agent continued as one of the other men came around and pulled Jackie's hands behind her back.

Jackie jerked her arm away. "I didn't do anything!" she repeated. They snapped handcuffs on her and began leading her toward the door. She looked at India, her eyes filled with desperation. "India, no, please."

India followed the agents to the door, trying desperately to keep her tears at bay.

"Please don't do this!" Jackie cried as they led her away. "I'm so sorry. We've been friends since we were ten. You can't do this!"

"I hope the money was worth it, Jackie." India slammed the door, then leaned against it and sank to the floor in tears.

39

Jackie was behind bars, but Julian was still loose. And the fact that Ava still couldn't get in touch with her sister gave her cause for concern.

She'd tried Mia's Los Angeles apartment and her cell phone countless times since she'd returned home last night. Just as Ava was trying to figure out her next move, her phone rang. Ava breathed a sigh of relief when she saw the number. She pressed the Talk button.

"Hey, sissy!" Mia sang.

"Don't 'sissy' me. Where have you been? I've been worried sick! One minute you're meeting with Julian, the next you're heading back to L.A. without so much as a call!"

"Umm, I sent you a text."

"That's not the same!" Ava chastised.

"Always the mother," Mia said. "But don't fret; I'm back in town."

"What do you mean you're back in town?

I thought you had to go back for a meeting?"

"I did. I met, now I'm back. This is major, so I caught a red-eye."

"What's major?" Ava said, a flash of panic sweeping over her. "What are you talking about? Where are you? Have you talked to Julian?"

"As a matter of fact, I have," Mia said. "Say hello, Julian."

"Hello, *sissy*." His gruff voice filled the phone and Ava felt her heart drop into the pit of her stomach.

Mia came back on the phone. "Yeah, he's taking me to meet with Sherri Shepherd from *The View*. She's a close friend of his and he told her all about me. She's no Barbara Walters, but how totally cool would it be if I were her personal assistant?"

"Mia, I need you to listen to me," Ava said sternly. Her heart was racing, and she needed to get her sister to stop rambling. "Julian is not what he seems."

"Oh, here you go again. Hold on," she said. It sounded like she was getting out of the car. There was a lot of rustling.

"Where are you?" Ava yelled.

"We're —"

Before she could finish, Julian came on the phone. "She's taken care of. That's all you need to worry about."

"Hey," Ava heard Mia say. "Why'd you snatch my phone?"

"Shut up, you annoying bitch," Julian snapped.

"Excuse me?"

Julian hissed into the phone. "You think you're slick, don't you? You should've listened to Fredericko and minded your own business."

"Julian, I swear to God, if you hurt my sister . . ."

"You'll what? You'll have a nice funeral for her, that's it."

"Put her back on the phone!" Ava screamed.

"No, I'm not putting her anywhere. I'm getting out of here, and she's my insurance to make that happen."

Tears filled Ava's eyes. "Julian, please. She's not in this. This is between me and you."

"What's going on?" Mia yelled in the background.

"Here, why don't you tell this brat what's going on?"

"Owww, you're hurting me," Mia cried. Her voice was clearer, so he must have put the phone back to her ear. "Why are you grabbing my arm?"

"Mia!" Ava said, trying to get her sister's attention. "I need you to listen to me. Julian was the one behind Felix's killing. He was the one behind everything with India."

"What are you talking about?"

"Where are you now?" Ava asked.

"We're at —"

Julian must have snatched the phone away. "Right now I have a gun in your sister's back. Unless you want me to pull the trigger, you will get me two hundred and fifty thousand dollars so I can get the hell out of Dodge."

"Two hundred and fifty thousand dollars? I don't have that kind of money."

"Call India. It's the least she can do for you," he said sarcastically. "I don't care how you get it. Just get it if you hope to ever see your sister alive again."

"Please don't hurt her," Ava sobbed.

"You should've thought about that before you went meddling where you didn't belong."

"Ava, help me," she heard her sister cry.

"Shut up!" It sounded like Julian slapped her as Mia screamed. "Get my money. I'm going to call you back in two hours. On a different phone. This one is going in the river, so don't bother trying to trace it. And no cops or I swear to God, I will put a bullet in her pretty little head." The phone went dead.

Ava's heart sank. How in the world would she find her sister? How would she get two hundred and fifty thousand dollars, and even if she did, would she get to her sister in time?

40

Ava did what she always did in times of crisis: she called Cliff. She could barely get her words out, she was crying so hard.

"Cl . . . Cliff," she cried.

"Ava, what's wrong?" As expected, the sound of her crying sent him into a panic.

Ava tried to calm herself down enough to talk. "It's Julian. He has Mia."

"What do you mean, he has Mia?" Cliff said.

"He kidnapped her and said I had to provide him with two hundred and fifty thousand dollars to leave town or he was going to kill her."

"You're not making sense, Ava. Calm down."

"Don't tell me to calm down!" Ava yelled. "That psycho has my sister. He told me if I call the cops, she's dead."

Cliff was silent, no doubt trying to process everything. "Okay, let me think," he said once she was done. "I know, does Mia have a cell phone?" He sounded like he was walking outside.

"Of course she does. But Julian said he was tossing it. Why?"

"Dang. We could've traced it to find out where she was."

Ava's eyes suddenly grew wide as she replayed her sister's words in her head. *Mr. Abernathy gave me this BlackBerry so he could have access to me at all times.* "She does have another phone. A company Black-Berry. Maybe she has that one on her."

"Well, hopefully she has it turned on. Do you have that number?"

Ava thought for a moment. She did remember her sister calling her from that number the other day. "Hold on, let me scroll through my phone." Ava placed Cliff on hold, then scrolled through the phone until she came across the 310 number. She immediately punched the number in. Her heart raced as she waited for the other end to pick up. Please God, let this be her phone.

"Hi, you've reached Mia Cole, the personal assistant to Mr. Abernathy. If your call —"

Ava didn't give the message time to finish as she clicked back over. "Cliff, I have the number!" She rattled off the number.

"Okay, got it," he said.

"But what about the money? Where am I supposed to get that kind of money?"

Cliff sighed heavily. "Look, I don't have two hundred and fifty, but I can get about one seventy-five. It's the money I had for my studio."

Ava fell onto her sofa. "Cliff, I can't take your money." She wanted to take the money and run, anything to save her sister, but she couldn't have this man give up his life dream.

"Hopefully we'll be able to stop Julian before he takes off with the money. Worst-case scenario, we'll sell the story to the *Star* and get the money back, okay?"

She knew he was trying to make her feel better, but her stomach remained in knots.

"Just trust me on this. I'll run by the bank and you meet me at the office so we can track Mia down. You know we have all kinds of high-tech gadgets there, including the GPS tracking system. How do you think we always know where the celebrities are? I'm going to call Victor, the guy who does our tracking."

Ava wiped away her tears, starting to feel a glimmer of hope. "Thank you, Cliff."

"There'll be plenty of time for you to

thank me later. Just come on."

Ava almost had a panic attack at how slow the cabbie was driving. Out of all the crazy cabbies in New York, she *would* get the one who wanted to obey all the traffic laws. "Sir," she said, leaning forward, "I really need to get to my destination. It's an emergency."

He pointed to the traffic and said, "What do you want me to do?"

"I'll give you an extra fifty dollars if you can get me there in the next fifteen minutes."

"Now you're speaking my language," he said. In a flash he whipped out into traffic, nearly colliding with another car. Ava hung on for dear life as he swerved in and out of the lanes of traffic. But true to his word, he pulled up in front of the *National Star* building in thirteen minutes.

"Thank you so much." She handed him the amount of the fare, plus fifty dollars.

She jumped out of the cab and raced toward the front door. She pulled out her phone and called Cliff. "Where are you?"

"I'm in the basement."

"I didn't know we had a basement."

"You're not supposed to know. Go around

to the service elevator and come all the way down."

"Okay, I'm on my way."

Ava's eyes goggled when the elevator doors opened up in the basement. It was like something out of a spy movie. All kinds of high-tech gadgets were lined up around the room. A long rectangular table housed seemingly everyday items. Ava spotted a woman's rhinestone belt, a serving tray, a couple of purses, a necktie, and an assortment of other personal items.

"What's all this stuff?" Ava asked as she approached Cliff.

"Every one of those items has a camera in it. You don't think the *Star* gets all of their pictures by a stroke of good luck, do you?" He pointed to a small door toward the back of the room. "Come on, Victor's in here, waiting on us. I've already given him your sister's number, and he's input it into the system. He's managed to narrow its location to a ten-block radius."

"But that could be anywhere."

"No, Victor is the best at what he does. He says he should be able to pinpoint a spot in about five minutes."

Cliff led her into a small room with even more high-tech stuff, including three large screens that had to be forty-two inches. On them were all kinds of data. It looked like a jumbled Google map. A dark-haired man sat slumped over a keyboard.

"Victor, Ava. Ava, Victor," Cliff said, though neither of them bothered to speak. "So, any more luck?" Cliff continued.

"Yeah." Victor zeroed in on a building on the screen. "The signal is coming from this area," he said, pointing to the screen.

"Great, then we call the cops," Ava said, reaching for the phone.

"Didn't he say no cops?" Cliff asked.

"Yeah, but I can't —"

"My point is, Julian isn't stupid. He's not going to show up with your sister just in case we do call the cops. We have to play this safe."

"So we're not calling the cops?" Ava asked.

"We will, but we have to find your sister first. I did call a friend on the force. He's on it but he can't make a move until I tell him."

Ava didn't know about that plan, but she knew that at this point, she trusted Cliff and she was willing to do whatever he said.

"Bingo! Got it," Victor said. "They are at 331 West Eleventh Street."

"Where are you supposed to meet him?"

Ava shrugged. "I don't know. He was going to call me. What if we're too late?" Ava felt tears welling up again.

"We won't be." Cliff hugged her. "Mia's going to be fine."

"My suggestion would be that Ava go meet him and you go grab the sister," Victor chimed in.

"That is a great idea," Ava said. "Cliff, you head over to the building where Mia is, and I'll go meet Julian."

"You are not going to go meet him by yourself!" Cliff firmly replied.

"There's no other way."

He shook his head vehemently. "No, you're not going by yourself!"

"Why don't I go?" Victor offered. "I've been longing for some action. I'm always stuck in this room."

Ava and Cliff exchanged glances. They didn't have much choice. It was either that or call the cops, and Ava didn't have time to explain everything to the police, wait for warrants, and so on. No, she needed to act now, and if Victor was the only way to make that happen, then Victor was on board.

"Fine, let's go."

41

Exactly ten minutes after they'd left the *National Star* offices, Ava's cell phone rang. It was an "unknown" number.

"Yes?" she said, the phone shaking in her hand.

"Meet me at the corner of Washington and Eleventh Street. Remember, no cops." That's all Julian said before the line went dead.

They had sent Victor on to the warehouse. As scared as she was, she still wondered if she should've come alone. She didn't need anything setting Julian off.

"This is it," Cliff said as they pulled up to an abandoned building. Cliff paid the taxi driver, then they slowly made their way inside. This place was scary with its boarded-up windows and dilapidated roofing.

"Julian!" Ava called out. Her voice echoed throughout the empty building.

"Did you come alone?" a voice called from down the long hallway.

"No, she didn't," Cliff immediately said, stepping into the room with Ava.

Julian laughed when Cliff emerged. "I see you brought your macho boyfriend."

"She did," Cliff replied. "You really didn't think I was going to let her come by herself."

Julian finally stepped out where they could see him. There was nothing handsome about him now. He wore a white jogging suit and was in desperate need of a shave. But what caught Ava's eye was the shiny black gun he had pointed their way.

"I knew she'd bring her hefty sidekick along."

"As long as you knew," Cliff said, his arm going protectively in front of Ava.

Never in a million years did Ava think that she'd be standing with a gym bag filled with money, in front of an armed man who had kidnapped her sister.

"Where are the cops?" Julian said.

"There are no cops," Ava replied. "It's just me."

"And me," Cliff added.

"Where'd you get the money?" Julian asked, eyeing the bag.

"Does it matter?" Ava said. "It didn't come from India, though. You didn't give me much time to track her down."

He motioned to the bag. "Is that all of it?"

"It is." She opened the bag and showed it to him. She was hoping he didn't take the time to count it. "Where is my sister?"

"Do you think I trust you? Just in case you decided to bring the cops along, I left her in a safe location. Sort of my insurance. If I get arrested, then you'll never know where your sister is."

Ava said a silent prayer that Victor had reached her sister. "Let me know that Mia is okay," Ava said.

"You just have to take my word for it," Julian said, jabbing the gun at Ava. "Now give me my money."

Ava leaned down and slid the bag toward him. Thankfully, Cliff had managed to get a lot of twenties and fifties along with hundreds, so the bag looked like two hundred and fifty thousand dollars, even though it wasn't.

Julian reached down, grabbed the bag, and laughed. "That's what I'm talking about," he said, running his hand through the bills.

"Where's my sister?" Ava repeated.

"Yeah, about that . . . I'll call you once I get settled and let you know." He zipped the bag up, then dashed out the side door.

"Julian! Where's my sister?" she screamed after him before turning to Cliff. "We haven't heard from Victor. What are we going to do? How do we know Victor found her?"

"Because he hasn't called, so we can only assume everything is fine," Cliff said reassuringly.

"I hope so. But Julian is gone with your money."

"Don't worry, he won't get far. Come on."

Ava followed Cliff downstairs. As they stepped outside, Julian was speeding out of the alleyway. As soon as his wheels hit the street, though, cops swarmed from everywhere, trapping Julian.

"Get out of the car with your hands up!" one officer yelled over a bullhorn.

Julian glared at Ava as he slowly stepped out of the car, his arms in the air.

Ava was just as shocked. "So you did call the cops?" she asked Cliff.

"Of course. I'm one tough dude, but I'm not stupid. I had my friend make sure they were on standby."

"But why didn't you tell me?"

Cliff was very pleased with himself. "The less you had to stress about, the better."

"You really messed up now," Julian called

out as they slammed him up against the car. "Now you'll never know where your sister is."

"I'm right here," Mia said wearily, coming around the corner. Her clothes were tattered and dirty and her hair stuck out all over her head. But to Ava, her sister had never looked more beautiful.

"Mia!" Ava said, racing to her and throwing her arms around her neck.

Mia hugged her sister tightly. "I don't know how you guys found me. I'm just glad you did."

Julian looked dumbfounded. "H-how did you get loose?"

"You are one dumb criminal," one of the officers said as he took Julian's hands and yanked them behind his back.

Ava patted her sister's face. "Are you sure you're okay?"

"I've been tied up in some stale-smelling building, starving to death. I just knew I was going to die in there," Mia said. "When I saw Victor, I thought he was coming to kill me."

Victor smiled. "Yeah, she actually fought me off for a minute, but when she saw me untying her, I guess she figured I was okay."

"Thank you so much, Ava," Mia said.

"Thank Cliff," Ava replied. "It seems the

Star is good for something." Ava explained how Victor had tracked her company cell phone, which Mia kept on vibrate, allowing him to pick up a signal and locate her.

By the time he finished, Mia looked totally impressed. "Well, you can hate that job all you want, Ava, but the *National Star* now has a fan for life." A new thought occurred to her. "Oooh, you think they'll be interested in buying my story?"

Laughing, Ava hugged her sister again. "I'm so glad you can joke after such an ordeal."

"Who's joking?"

They all laughed as the cops threw Julian into the back of the squad car.

42

Ava read the headline for the tenth time. FORMER SUPER STAR MANAGER PLEADS GUILTY. She sighed in relief and tucked the paper back in her bag. It was hard to believe that only six weeks had passed since Jackie and Julian had been arrested. After a scant few hours behind bars Jackie had been ready to prove she was indeed a talented singer — because she sang like a canary, telling everything she knew about Julian's plan to steal all of India's money. She even led police to the gun Julian had used to kill Felix.

Jackie's testimony provided an open-and-shut case to convict Julian, so he'd saved the expense and embarrassment of a trial and pled guilty. He hadn't been sentenced yet, but Ava was sure he would spend a long time behind bars.

To prove the adage that there's no such thing as bad publicity, the news of Julian's arrest had catapulted India's career to even greater heights. She made her rounds on the talk-show circuit, showing remorse for hiring a man who turned out to be a vicious criminal. All of the hosts exclaimed that even a famous pop star could be a victim of foul play.

Fredericko was out on bail. He'd been cleared of murder, but he was still facing grand larceny charges. India believed he would jump bail and move to another country — and find another woman to con. Ava agreed. She didn't think the world had heard the last of Fredericko de la Cruz.

"So what are you going to do now?" India asked as she pulled out her credit card to pay the bill. The two of them were at lunch at a bistro off Fifth Avenue. India had been superbusy for the last few weeks, but had called Ava to meet for lunch to thank her once again for everything that she had done.

Ava shrugged. "That's the million-dollar question. I have no idea what I'm going to do. I just know that I can't do the paparazzi thing." That had been the kicker in all of this. Despite all the accolades she'd received from her boss, Ava simply couldn't continue digging up dirt on celebrities. She'd covered five other celebrity scandal stories since India, and each one made her sicker than the last. She'd heard the "they decided to go in a different direction" spiel from the network, and she couldn't help but chalk that up to all of the negative publicity surrounding India's story. "I haven't turned in my resignation yet because I have to figure out a way to have some money coming in, but I'm definitely working on an exit plan. I know that when all is said and done, I have to tell myself that I was put on this earth for a calling greater than this."

"Hey, I would have to agree with you there," India said, handing the waiter the bill and her credit card.

Ava leaned back in her seat. "What about you? I know you're busy with the new album and new movie. Denzel and Brad? You have to be the luckiest woman alive."

India laughed. "Yeah, and to think I was two seconds from passing up on it because of all this drama. Still, my true passion is getting this foundation off the ground."

"Yeah, I think that the foundation in Kaitlyn's honor is a phenomenal idea."

"It's definitely near and dear to my heart. I may not have been directly responsible for the accident that killed Kaitlyn, but in a way, I still feel like I am responsible for her death. If Julian hadn't taken us to the party, if I hadn't had too much to drink . . ." Her voice trailed off.

"We all can learn a lot from ifs," Ava said.

A smile crossed India's face. "You're right about that." She signed the receipt the waiter had set in front of her, then leaned back like a thought had just come to her. "Hey, I have an idea. Someone approached me about writing my life story. Obviously, I don't have time, so I was thinking, are you interested in being a ghostwriter?"

"I'm interested in anything that pays the bills." Ava laughed.

"It's a really good offer from the publisher," India said. "How about I have my new manager give you a call?"

"I'd like that." Ava couldn't believe her luck. She'd prayed for a way out, and just like that, her prayers had been answered.

India's eyes drifted out into the street. "Ummm, I think your knight in shining armor awaits you," she said, pointing to Cliff, who was leaning against his truck outside the patio area where they were having lunch.

"Yeah, he insisted on picking me up. We're taking a couple of days and traveling out of the city — you know, just to get away." Ava smiled lovingly. Cliff waved and mouthed, *Take your time. I'll be right here.*

"He's a little protective," Ava added, turning back to India. "But I like it." That had been the best thing to come out of all this — her relationship with Cliff. They'd become friends and lovers. There was no talk of marriage — yet — but Cliff had definitely turned out to be the man of her dreams.

"Well, count your blessings, girl," India said. "What I wouldn't give to have someone protect me right about now. You hold him tight because a good man is hard to find."

Ava looked back over her shoulder and smiled. "Don't I know it. And now that I found one, you can believe I'm never letting go."